THIS IS NOT A DRILL

BECK McDOWELL

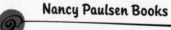

Nancy Paulsen Books

An Imprint of Penguin Group (USA) Inc.

YA
McD
C4

NANCY PAULSEN BOOKS • A division of Penguin Young Readers Group.
Published by The Penguin Group.
Penguin Group (USA) Inc., 375 Hudson Street, New York, NY 10014, U.S.A.
Penguin Group (Canada), 90 Eglinton Avenue East, Suite 700, Toronto, Ontario M4P 2Y3, Canada
(a division of Pearson Penguin Canada Inc.).
Penguin Books Ltd, 80 Strand, London WC2R 0RL, England.
Penguin Ireland, 25 St. Stephen's Green, Dublin 2, Ireland
(a division of Penguin Books Ltd).
Penguin Group (Australia), 250 Camberwell Road, Camberwell, Victoria 3124, Australia
(a division of Pearson Australia Group Pty Ltd).
Penguin Books India Pvt Ltd, 11 Community Centre, Panchsheel Park, New Delhi—110 017, India.
Penguin Group (NZ), 67 Apollo Drive, Rosedale, Auckland 0632, New Zealand
(a division of Pearson New Zealand Ltd).
Penguin Books (South Africa) (Pty) Ltd, 24 Sturdee Avenue,
Rosebank, Johannesburg 2196, South Africa.
Penguin Books Ltd, Registered Offices: 80 Strand, London WC2R 0RL, England.

Published simultaneously in Canada. Printed in the United States of America.
Design by Marikka Tamura. Text set in Carré Noir Std.

Library of Congress Cataloging-in-Publication Data
McDowell, Rebecca.
This is not a drill / Rebecca McDowell.   p. cm.
Summary: "Two teens must work together to protect a class of first-graders when a soldier
with post-traumatic stress disorder takes them hostage"—Provided by publisher.
[1. Post-traumatic stress disorder—Fiction. 2. Hostages—Fiction. 3. Survival—Fiction.
4. Schools—Fiction. 5. Family problems—Fiction.] I. Title.
PZ7.M15835Thi 2012   [Fic]—dc23   2012011083

ISBN 978-0-399-25794-0
1   3   5   7   9   10   8   6   4   2

*This book is dedicated to the memory of
the Rev. Dr. J. L. Brigman,
who read me countless books, sang me to sleep,
pressed fall leaves between waxed paper,
and loved us like crazy for as long as he could.*

CHAPTER 1

Emery

Night seeps through the hospital blinds. I can't stop shivering as I pull the blanket the nurse gave me around my shoulders. I'm so tired, but every time I close my eyes, I see that terrible image—the image of the first graders blinking in shock at the gun pointed at their teacher's head.

It didn't belong there, between the word wall and the vowel sounds chart. It was like that game in the Sunday cartoon section where you search for the tiny mistakes added to the picture. Only this mistake wasn't tiny; it was a silent explosion that ate up the oxygen in the room and turned the warm yeasty air ice-cold.

We started class this morning with our lesson on French words for animals.

And by the afternoon, three people were dead.

The calendar on the wall in Intensive Care says

Friday, November 5. A long day that taught me a lot. About life. And love. And myself.

The truth is, I'd never have signed up to teach French to elementary school kids three mornings a week if I'd known I'd get partnered with Jake Willoughby—after what he did to me. But Mrs. Campbell, the first grade teacher, was so cool, she made everything easier. When I told her I'd always wanted to teach, she took me under her wing. She told me and Jake, "I like the way you keep the children's interest. It's going to be a smooth semester for you two." She was being nice, but still, it makes me nervous when people make predictions about good things without knocking on wood—because it's kind of like asking for it, in a way.

But I can't blame her. Mrs. Campbell couldn't have stopped what was going to happen. No one could have. From the minute Brian Stutts stepped into the room, that train had left the station.

I keep going back to the beginning—looking for where we went wrong, what we could have done differently. I need to retrace our steps, because if I don't know what to look for, it could happen again, couldn't it? Death finding us on an ordinary day.

An ordinary day that started like this:

The kids lean forward in their chairs, jumping at each new flash card, everybody wanting to be the first to yell the animal's French name and sound. It's early in the day, but fall sweaters have already been shed in the November sun that pours through the windows.

The first graders love it that the sounds animals make are different in other languages. When I tell them that a French pig says *groin, groin* instead of *oink, oink*, DeQuan starts saying it over and over again until I make him stop. (I'm pretty sure no pig ever said *oink, oink*—even though *groin, groin* isn't much better.)

"*Qu'est-ce que c'est?*" I ask as Jake holds up the flash card cat I made from coloring book pages.

"*C'est un chat,*" the first graders singsong, just like we taught them. Redheaded Alicia's voice is louder than everyone else's. They learn so fast—like an adorable bunch of little sponges.

Natalie waves her hand frantically.

"Yes, Natalie?"

"Miss Emery, my daddy got mad at my mommy and broked a lamp; it was a big one and he threw it at the wall and it broked into little pieces."

"I'm sorry to hear that, sweetie. Can we talk about it later?" I say. First graders tell everything—to everyone—all the time. And Natalie loves drama. With her long reddish-blond hair and freckles, she's like a mini Lindsay Lohan, only with two front teeth missing.

I point to the picture of a dog Jake's holding up. "*Qu'est-ce que c'est, classe?*"

"That's my sister," yells Mason Mayfield III. I give him a

look. I'm learning that it takes a lot of looks to keep Mason Mayfield III in line.

"*C'est un chien,*" seventeen others call out. They dance in their seats, an arm-flapping, foot-tapping sea of energy.

"*Très bien,*" I say to them with a smile, glancing at Mrs. Campbell at her desk in front. She always tells them they're doing great, even on days when they aren't. She says it's a self-fulfilling prophecy. If you say they're getting it, they really will. The kids love her. Even her perfume is kid-friendly; she smells like grass and sunlight. She has the Animal Kingdom eating out of her hand. Jake, too, I've noticed.

"*Qu'est-ce que c'est?*" I ask the kids as Jake holds up a picture of a cow.

Before they can answer, a loud knock on the door makes everyone jump.

"What the—?" Mason Mayfield III says. All heads turn to the little round window, now filled with a man's face—all squinty eyes and angry frown.

Mrs. Campbell is barely out of her seat when the door swings open and the man walks in like he owns the place: big guy, late twentyish, dark hair buzzed close, square jaw. Black T-shirt stretched tight across puffed-out chest. Muscular legs in camouflage pants. Army boots planted wide.

His eyes scan the kids' faces like he's searching for a tasty meal. His focus stops on one.

"Can I help you?" Mrs. Campbell's desk is on the wall opposite the door, but she crosses the room in a flash and stops him before he gets too far inside. He might be a soldier, but this is her territory.

"Yeah. I'm Brian Stutts. I came to get my son, Patrick." All eyes turn to Patrick Stutts. In the back of the room, he shrinks in his seat, pinned by his father's glare and his classmates' curious stares. Patrick looks down, his head tucked in his usual pose, chin on chest. He speaks in whispers and often hums to himself, lost in his own world. I've tried hard to draw him out of his shell, but without much success.

"I'm sorry, Mr. Stutts, but checkouts are done through the front office." Mrs. Campbell's voice is polite, but stern. "You're really not allowed to come to the classroom."

"I want my kid. Patrick, come on. We're going." He jerks his head toward the door, exposing lizard talons that creep up his neck, tattooed claws reaching from his shirt for his jutting jaw and square head.

"Oooo-eee." DeQuan reacts under his breath, his eyes round.

"Mr. Stutts, you'll need to return to the front office and go through the proper channels to check out your son. Let me show you the way." Mrs. Campbell somehow herds the big man into the hall and, miraculously, he allows himself to be ushered out. She closes the door behind her as she talks to him softly, her eyes locked on his. I swear the woman could have been a lion tamer. She actually looks a little like Reese Witherspoon in that circus movie.

I'm not aware that I've been holding my breath until I let

it out when he leaves. His departure is a relief to the kids, too.

"Did you see that—" DeQuan says, but I cut him off with a frown and a head shake. "But Miss Emery, it was comin' outta his shirt and it had claws—"

"DeQuan," I say, stopping him.

"Was *that* Patrick's daddy?" Alicia asks.

The kids stare at the top of Patrick's drooping head. Rose, bless her heart, leans over and plops a handful of floppy fur in front of him—the worn-out stuffed animal she calls Lamby, who travels with her everywhere.

"So, guys," Jake recovers for us, "we were on this one." He holds up the cow and looks at me, running a hand through his dark hair nervously. He's rarely ever rattled.

I take his cue to get things back on track. "Okay, pay attention, everyone."

When Mrs. Campbell walks calmly back into the room, the class visibly relaxes. She sits down and reaches for a pen, then looks up at the kids with an all's-right-with-the-world smile.

I wonder how many crazy parents she's dealt with. There's not much protection from anyone who wants to come into the building. The elementary school hired a security guard last year after a homeless guy was caught in the parking lot "displaying his wares," as my mom called it. The guy who's usually in the front hall looks more like a grocery store bag boy than a cop. He sits at a table, texting on his phone, and barely looks up when we pass.

I grew up with an unhealthy dose of "stranger danger." My helicopter mom's so overprotective, she used to read me kidnapping stories from the paper to scare me into staying close to her. It worked. I became glued to her side if anyone unfamiliar came near us. And I even planned out how I'd get away if I got captured like Elizabeth Smart.

I was so shy in elementary school that the other kids called me Whisper Girl. While they chased each other at recess, I leaned against the big tree at the edge of the playground, half hiding, and watched. In third grade, the teacher had to make a rule that no one could speak for me to stop my classmates from filling in my silence.

The panic attacks started in middle school—at least that's what we called them then, the embarrassing episodes of dizziness and short breath that got worse as people started staring at me. I felt like a freak until I finally found a doctor last year who figured out how to help me. It turned out my problems went much deeper than shyness and anxiety. I've learned to control my symptoms now, but stress causes all my reflexes to go haywire. Mr. Stutts is not helping one little bit.

The kids smile back at Mrs. C., then they look blankly at us, their concentration broken. Lewis, the class roamer, is out of his seat, making googly eyes and bubble mouths at the fish in the tank.

"Lewis, will you join us, please?" I use Mrs. Campbell's favorite line for anyone who's drifting away—literally or mentally. I'm learning to speak authoritatively; Mrs. C. says I have to compensate for my soft voice ("tone, not volume") if I want the kids to take me seriously. Lewis looks at me and slinks back to his seat.

"Okay, everybody, *qu'est-ce que c'est?*" I have just begun again when—*BANG!*—the door swings open, this time with a force that sends it slamming into the wall. Everyone jumps, and all eyes are riveted on the angry giant in the doorway.

"I'm taking my kid, and you can't stop me," he sneers at Mrs. Campbell.

"Mr. Stutts, I'm afraid I'm going to have to insist—"

"I'm not going to the office. Those people just wanna keep my son from me. They're on *her* side."

"Mr. Stutts, please . . ." Mrs. Campbell stands up, but Stutts holds up a warning hand.

"Stand back, lady. Patrick, get your things. We're going."

"Mr. Stutts, if you don't return to the front office, I'll have to call security." Mrs. Campbell starts toward the phone on the wall. The big man snorts—apparently as unimpressed with security as we were.

And then it happens. Just as Mrs. Campbell reaches for the phone, before anyone realizes what he's doing, Stutts strides across the room, grabs the phone, and rips it off the wall. The plastic casing cracks, and we stare at the wires dangling from his huge hand. He turns and glares at Mrs. Campbell. My stomach flops with a sick twinge—the kind you have as a kid when your balloon flies out of your hands and you know you can't get it back.

"I don't think that'll be necessary, Teacher," he says. We all stare at him, holding the ruin of the phone with his shoulders reared back and a look of triumph on his face.

"Emery, will you walk down to the office," Mrs. Campbell says without taking her eyes off him, "and ask Mrs. Bishop to—"

I take a step toward the door, but Stutts lunges forward and grabs my arm with his free hand—a hard, painful grip that makes me wince.

"Hey, don't—" Jake moves toward us, but stops when Stutts wheels to face him, twisting my arm harder as a warning. I press my lips together to keep from crying out.

My brain registers the sweetish smell of alcohol on the man's breath. It's nine o'clock in the morning.

"Stay right where you are—both of you," he orders.

I try to pull away. I don't want this guy touching me.

"Emery." Jake says my name quietly, and when I turn to him, his calm blue eyes hold mine for a second. I stop struggling and Stutts lets go. Jake steps closer to me and reaches out to pull me toward him. An odd thought surfaces from the rushing current of my brain—it's the first time I've let Jake touch me in months.

"Patrick, get your things," Stutts says again. Patrick reaches for the backpack hanging on his chair.

"Patrick, sit down," Mrs. Campbell says in a surprisingly

steady voice. "You're not leaving without permission from the office." Poor Patrick looks at her, hesitates, then sinks back in his seat and puts his head on his desk with his arms crossed above it, his face hidden.

"Don't tell my boy what to do," the man growls. "Nobody tells my boy what to do but me."

"Mr. Stutts, I'll be happy to walk with you down to the office," Mrs. Campbell says as she moves toward the door. "We can—"

"Stop right there." He drops the phone with a clatter and reaches into one of the pockets of his camo pants. My eyes follow the cordlike veins leading down from his bulging biceps. He raises his fist.

Gripping a handgun.

Aimed directly at the teacher.

The first graders freeze—almost as if they're posing for some weird yearbook picture. No one moves.

Jake's hand tightens on my arm.

This isn't real.

It has to be a toy. Some kind of sick joke.

Things like this don't happen in our sleepy little town. In Hensonville, a new traffic light is a big event. Things like this belong on CNN. My head feels light and the room tilts a little.

Mrs. Campbell inhales sharply. Her eyes move from the gun to Stutts's face. She slowly holds up her hands like in the movies and says, "Mr. Stutts, please put that away so we can talk." Her teacher-voice has gone trembly. "I'm sure we can resolve this without resorting to . . ." Her voice trails off, but the word *violence* floats in the air with the specks of dust suspended in the slanting morning rays.

And then, for the life of me, I can't tell you what makes me do it. In a move that's totally uncharacteristic of me, I pull away from Jake and take a step toward Stutts.

"No," I say without any thought besides making this go away. "Don't do this. You can't—"

"You want a piece of this?" Stutts yells—turning to point his weapon *straight at me*.

My stomach turns inside out as I stare down the barrel of the gun. All I can think is—*my mother was right. I'm going to die at the hands of a homicidal maniac. Her warnings about strangers have finally come true.*

CHAPTER 2

JAKE

I SWEAR IT'S ONE OF THE HARDEST things I've ever done—keeping still. And what's up with Emery, arguing with this guy? As much as I want to jump him, I know it's insanity to take on a man with a gun.

It's one of those situations where any wrong move can send things in a direction I don't want to think about. My dad calls it the Law of Unintended Consequences—you can't predict the chain reaction of disaster one small deed can set in motion, so you have to think before you act.

I know it's better to feel like a wuss than to do the wrong thing, but it really pisses me off, this guy coming into a room full of little kids and pulling a stunt like this. What kinda freak does that? These kids are gonna need therapy for the rest of their lives. Hell, *I* might need therapy—shit'll mess you up.

"Mr. Stutts, you're going to cause yourself a lot of problems," Mrs. Campbell says. "This isn't going to—"

"Just shut up!" he yells. "Shut up so I can think."

I calculate the distance between me and the gun, even though I know it's not worth the risk. I can't do anything that might hurt Emery, the teacher, or these kids. They're watching us, counting on us to help them, but all we can do is wait silently for Stutts's next move.

Before we started teaching here, little kids really got on my nerves. Like those obnoxious brats in those skate shoes—Heelys—that come at you in the mall like flying monkeys from *The Wizard of Oz* and then swerve around you at the last minute? I freakin' hate that.

I only signed on for tutoring because, on the two days a week you're not at the elementary school, the French teacher doesn't really expect you to show up in class—kind of an understood senior perk. In my book, a sleeping-in privilege is a big incentive to do anything.

I didn't think Mrs. Sherrill was gonna let me do it at first. She's always on my case for not doing my French homework. I had to turn on the charm to convince her to let me tutor. She finally agreed, but I wouldn't be her pick to defend a bunch of first graders against a nutjob with a handgun—especially after my run-in with the local po-lice this summer.

Hell, I wouldn't be my pick, either. Anytime a school shooting story comes on the news, I always think about what I'd do if I was there. I wanna believe the next-day headlines would read High School Student Saves Lives of Classmates. I always hope I'd be the guy who leaps in front of the speeding bullet to save the beautiful girl. Or at least maybe the dude who talks the bad guy down and gets him to hand over his weapon. Okay, I'm not gonna lie—I just don't wanna be the kid who crawls out from under a desk with pee stains on the front of his pants after the shooter leaves the building.

My dad says I'm "untrustworthy and irresponsible." It's a pretty widely held opinion in this town since my recent arrest. But I'm betting even my dad would agree that I'm doing the responsible thing right now—nothing. I've never been face-to-face with a guy with a gun before, but I know right from the start there isn't much I *can* do. This dude is well over six feet tall, probably 240 pounds, neck the size of my thigh—and ready to back up any threat he makes.

It's not something we talk about, but when guys walk in a room, we do this quick, practically subconscious scan of every guy there: If a fight broke out, who could I take and who would I have to watch out for? It happens in a flash—kind of a survival-of-the-fittest thing.

It's not like I'm a total lightweight. I'm right at six feet myself, I stay in shape for baseball, and I work on my uncle's farm in the summer and on weekends bailing hay and hauling heavy shit. But this guy is hardcore, man—in every way. Hell, he probably has *Kill* tattooed inside his bottom lip. He's got that crazy roid rage look in his eye, the one that says *Bring it, you pathetic peon. Give me one good reason to bash your head in with my bare hands.* I've always been pretty good at reading people's faces, and what I see in this guy's eyes is damn scary.

Bottom line, there's no way to make this right. I've always been good at fixin' broken stuff. I'd rather work on cars and take lawn mower engines apart than make straight A's like my older brother. Stephen's the brain of the family, and I'm the hands-on guy. At least, that's what I tell my dad when he gets on me about grades. But this time, hands-on won't work. I can't MacGyver my way out with a weapon made from an eraser and a rubber band. All I can do is wait for Stutts to show me his next move—and pray that his finger on the trigger is steady.

The fear in Emery's pale green eyes just about kills me. Emery's solid; she's the real deal. Most girls don't stack up to your expectations in the end—kinda like those movies everybody raves about and then when you finally see them, you're disappointed. But Emery was every bit as cool as I thought she'd be. Her mind is lightning fast, and her mouth is always curled up at the corners like she's thinking about some private joke.

The first time I really talked to her was in art class. I sat in the seat next to her and tried to make eye contact. She ignored me. So I reached over and picked up the camera she was using for a photography project, put my face next to hers, and turned it around to take a picture of the two of us. She still ignored me. Finally I leaned over and whispered, "So, I hear you think I'm an asshole."

"I didn't say you were an asshole," she said, turning red.

"I said you were conceited. And it's true." She smiled—that great smile of hers that starts as a wicked grin and spreads—and then she turned back to Molly like I didn't exist, which, of course, really chapped my ass. So I quit talking to her.

"What's the matter, Biscuit, got your feelings hurt?" she asked me a few minutes later, grinning. I stop at Hardee's every day on the way to school for a butter biscuit and eat it before class starts, so I knew she was making fun of me, but I didn't mind.

There's tons of downtime in art class, so we wound up talking a bunch that day. Emery's really funny, but half the stuff she says is under her breath, so you have to listen close to catch it. She made me laugh so hard, I got in trouble with the teacher and had to stay for detention. I don't even re-member what we were laughing about.

After school my buddy Cole said, "I heard you were hav-ing a big conversation with Emery Austin. She's not really your type."

"You mean smart, Cole?" I asked. "You think smart's not my type?"

"She's president of the damn Honor Society, for God's sake."

"And your point is?"

"Whatever, man."

The thing is, I wanted to be the kind of guy a girl like Emery Austin could go for. A girl who's smart and funny like my mom was before she got sick. Being with Emery re-minded me of who I was—or who I used to be. When we lost Mom, I got kind of lost, too, for a while. I stopped caring—about everything. I thought there was no use in being a good person without her watching. It's like the me that used to be was mostly about her, and once she was gone, there wasn't much reason to try.

Stutts doesn't move. The kids are completely still, which is a miracle, 'cause usually just getting them in their seats is like trying to nail Jell-O to the wall. Even Mason Mayfield III is stone-cold silent, and Lewis is in his chair, motionless.

A horn honks outside, and a door slams down the hall somewhere. The hamster suddenly starts going crazy on his little wheel in the back of the room, like he knows something's up. The kids named him Mr. Worley after their favorite janitor who just retired.

"Hey, you!" Stutts yells at me.

"Jake," I tell him. "My name is Jake."

"Yeah, whatever. I need you to empty your pockets."

"What for?" I ask.

"Maybe you got a pocketknife," he says. "I don't want you gettin' any smart ideas."

"All I have on me is some change—and my wallet."

"Turn 'em out anyway."

I pretend to empty my pockets onto the desk nearest me, hoping he won't notice the slight cell phone bulge still there. "Don't worry," I tell him. "You won't have any problem from me. I don't want these kids hurt, and besides, I'm no hero." That's the understatement of the year.

"I don't wanna hurt anybody, either, kid. I'm just tryin' to be a good dad. I'm not gonna let them take my son away from me. Not my wife"—he's getting louder and some of his words are slurred—"and not a bunch of small-town bureaucrats like those people down in the office. I don't need anybody tryin' to run my life. You got that, *Jake*?"

"We'll do whatever we can to help you, sir," I say, keeping my voice even and looking him in the eye. "Just don't hurt the people in this room. We're not your enemy."

"That's the problem, *Jake*; I don't know who the enemy is anymore. Maybe I *never* knew who the enemy was. The enemy's everywhere." His voice gets even louder. "You don't know who's tryin' to mess you up. You can't tell where the shootin's comin' from!"

It's crazy talk so I keep quiet. Emery's eyes move from the gun aimed at her to Stutts and back to the gun again. The gun changes everything, and there's no way to know how this will end.

CHAPTER 3
Emery

"If you put that away, Mr. Stutts, I promise you," Mrs. Campbell says soothingly, "we'll meet with the principal to get to the bottom of whatever problems you're having with the school." I notice she doesn't say the word *gun*.

I can see Jake's fists clench, and I'm praying he doesn't try to rush this guy.

"I talked with that lady in the office yesterday. I know what my wife's told them. You know damn well there's not gonna be any meeting."

"Mr. Stutts, *please* . . . the *children*." I realize she's warning him about his language—a man holding a gun—and I almost laugh.

"There's nothing to talk about. I'm taking my kid."

He moves toward Patrick, lowering the gun a little, but Mrs. Campbell steps between them. Rose's chair makes a sudden scraping sound as she scoots closer to Patrick, her dark eyes solemn.

Patrick looks up at her gratefully, picks up Lamby, and tucks the floppy animal under his arm.

"Lady, you better get out of my way," Stutts growls at Mrs. Campbell. He aims the gun back at her, and I feel a twinge of guilt that I'm happy it's not aimed at me anymore. She doesn't look at it, but I can't look at anything else.

"These children are my responsibility." Mrs. Campbell lowers her voice. It's what she does when she wants to get the kids' attention. If it's something really important, she speaks almost in a whisper and everyone in the room stops to listen. The screamer who teaches across the hall could take a lesson. "I'm not letting any of them leave the room without authorization from the office," she says, "and I'm certainly not letting them leave with someone who is armed."

I glance toward the open door, hoping *someone* will walk past and see the man with a gun standing in the middle of the neatly stacked red plastic boxes of math toys, the BRUSH YOUR TEETH posters, and the alphabet letters penciled on Big Chief paper. I look around at the kids and wonder if they can hear my heart hammering. Sweet babies, they look so confused. I wish I could cover their eyes like moms do during scary parts of movies.

Simon watches the gun through his big thick glasses with eyes that miss nothing. Alicia moves closer to tiny, apple-cheeked Kimberly with her springy dark curls. Janita pulls at her top lip beneath the self-inflicted haircut that left her bangs uneven. Patrick hunches his shoulders and rocks back and forth, and Kenji, on Patrick's other side, whispers something to him. Lewis pulls the neck of his shirt up over his nose so his eyes peek out like a turtle head.

The first week we were here was like a *South Park* episode. Natalie threw up, Mason Mayfield III got sent to the office for stabbing Tyler with a pencil, Carlos had a nosebleed that left a trail on the floor to the bathroom, and it took three days to track down a bad smell that turned out to be a rotten banana Kenji left in a bag tucked in the bookcase. Oh, and DeQuan stepped on Mr. Worley when he got out of his cage; fortunately, he survived. And when Simon saw Natalie throw up, he threw up, too.

Mason Mayfield III is the original high-maintenance kid, all the way down to his name, which seems to require all its parts whenever you speak of him.

"Hey, do you know my cousin, Mark Mayfield?" he asked us the first day, waving his hand like a maniac. "He goes to Hensonville High, too. He's the quarterback." He said it like he was saying *He's the pope.*

I've heard Jake refer to Mark Mayfield as "one of the biggest dicks around," but I was pretty sure he would know this was not the time to bring that up.

"I do know Mark. I can see the resemblance," Jake answered, winking at me. *Wicked cute wink,* my heart said. *Wicked bad boy,* my brain reminded me. I was not about to get blindsided by Jake Willoughby's charm again. It's taken me months to get that wink, that killer smile, that deep teasing voice out of my head.

These kids make me more sure than ever that I want to teach. They're so incredibly cute with their big round eyes and wide baby foreheads and turned up noses. We learned in biology that infants are born that way to bring out the protective instincts of adults. Baby animals have the same kinds of features on their furry kitten and bunny faces so you can't turn them down when they need food or affection.

The kids treated us like rock stars from the minute we arrived, asking a million questions about our pets, siblings, and favorite TV shows, listening wide-eyed to everything we said. Rose especially followed Jake around, smiling up at him like he just finished hanging the moon.

"Is that you?" I asked, peering over his shoulder at a drawing she handed him on our way out one day that first week. It was a picture of a tall dark-haired stick boy with bright blue eyes. There were hearts coming out of the boy's head. "Someone has a crush," I said, laughing.

"Rose? She's really cute."

"You remember her name; I'm impressed." It came out snarkier than I meant it. I had actually been making an attempt to get along since we were stuck with each other three times a week for an entire semester. I mean, I needed to show him I'm really over him.

And I was.

I am.

"I'm actually pretty decent with names, you know," Jake said. "Must be the political gene."

"Ah, the mayor's son works the crowd," I said. "How is the city's chief executive?"

"Great. You know how he loves life in the fishbowl."

"It's not without its perks, you have to admit."

"Pretty damn few." He frowned. "In exchange for a few free tickets to stuff now and then, I'm under constant inspection by every soccer mom and little old lady with a vote to cast. Like an ant under a magnifying glass—always getting burned."

I shifted my backpack, heavy with extra books I'd brought to show the kids pictures of France, and he reached out to take it. Jake Willoughby is very considerate when he wants to be. I'll give him that.

We walked through the bright yellow elementary school hallway that smelled of old books, overcooked vegetables, dusty cabinets, and dirty socks.

"Sometimes I play a little game," Jake said. "I do something I shouldn't just to see how long it will take to get back to my dad."

"And?"

"The record is ten minutes, but the average is about two hours."

"I heard about the drug charge." I lowered my voice as we passed an older kid swinging a hall pass on an elastic cord.

"Who hasn't? It's not like you think, Emery." His eyes clouded. "It wasn't my weed."

"It's really not my business," I said with a shrug. And it wasn't. I mean, I cared what happened to him like you'd care about any friend—not that we were friends anymore, but you don't just turn your back on people who were once important to you.

Even if they do turn out to be unworthy of your trust.

He didn't elaborate, and I didn't ask. If it wasn't his weed, I knew he wouldn't rat out a friend. Especially if the friend was Cole. I'm not a Cole fan. He's shallow and self-centered, and he turns everything into a big joke. I've never understood why Jake is friends with him.

"I know it was stupid," Jake said. "You don't have to say it."

"I wasn't going to." I was tempted to say it's not the first stupid thing he's done. But we'd reached the front of the building, so I held out my hand for my backpack.

"Look, Emery, I'm really sorry about what happened—you know, between us."

I held up my hand to stop him. "Over and done with." Not going there. *So* not going there.

Jake saw my face and backed off. "Hey, I just wanted to say thanks—for putting up with me as a tutoring partner. I know it's not what you wanted." He was making it hard to stay mad, smiling down at me with that charming country-boy grin set in a lean face bronzed from working in the sun.

"No big deal. It's not like I had a choice," I said.

"The kids are really into the lessons you put together. You're so great with them," he said.

It was obvious Jake wanted to talk. I was suddenly finding it hard to breathe.

"I . . . I gotta go," I said, moving toward my getaway vehicle.

"Sure, no problem. Hey, we could ride together tomorrow if you want."

"Maybe later, Jake." I walked toward my car quickly then, taking shallow gulps of air to hold my insides together, knowing that something was about to fly apart. I drove away fast so he wouldn't see the gush of tears when the dam crumbled, blurring my vision and shaking my faith in myself.

Stutts holds the gun out in front of him, still aimed at Mrs. Campbell. Jake makes a small step toward him and Stutts yells, "Everybody stay right where you are! Nobody moves till my kid and I are out of here."

Jake freezes and looks calmly at Stutts. Either he's much braver than I am or he's putting on a really good show for the kids.

"You're a *bad, bad* man!" Mason Mayfield III suddenly yells at Stutts, stomping his foot.

Stutts's face turns purple and he takes a menacing step toward Mason.

Mrs. Campbell moves to Mason's side at lightning speed. "Mason, no!" She grabs him by the shoulders.

"Hey, he's just a little kid," Jake says. "He doesn't mean anything. He just talks a lot."

"Shut him up!" Stutts shouts. "That kid doesn't know anything about me—and neither do you."

Mason Mayfield III crosses his arms and pouts as Mrs. Campbell talks quietly to him. He's obviously not getting it.

"Alla you kids keep your mouths shut and nobody'll get hurt," Stutts shouts, glaring at the rest of them.

Kimberly starts to cry and I move to comfort her. "Don't worry, sweetheart, it'll be okay," I whisper.

I look back at the other kids. They sit at eighteen small tabletop desks with tiny chairs; Mrs. Campbell usually groups them in pairs or fours. Patrick's head is ducked so low, his nose almost touches his desk, and Kenji leans over to whisper to him, his almond eyes full of concern. DeQuan is sucking his thumb, Alicia shakes her head slowly, and Lewis pulls his hands inside his sleeves and flaps them nervously. Rose reaches up to tug on a piece of her straight, dark hair, watching Jake through adoring eyes.

Their faces are puzzled. How can they possibly understand what's happening? We make sure they use blunt scissors to cut things and stop them from running on the playground. But we never prepared them for this. Even my mother's obsessive vigilance couldn't have kept these children safe if the simple act of going to school results in *this*.

And I don't know how to help them. I'm seventeen years old. I just wanted to teach little kids some French. I didn't sign on for dealing with a psycho.

I'm praying God's tuned in on this channel right now. I don't ask him for a lot; I figure he's busy. Right now I'm hoping I've saved up enough Good Girl Points to trade in for a big favor, because we're going to need all the help we can get if we're going to get out of this mess alive.

CHAPTER 4

JAKE

"YOU! DON'T MOVE! DON'T EVEN think about it!" the guy yells in my face. His whiskey breath could melt the metal on that gun.

"Sir, I'm going to do exactly what you want me to do," I answer, sending out respect vibes for all I'm worth. "Just don't hurt the kids."

"What I *want* you to do is stay out of my business," he practically spits at me. He wheels around to Mrs. Campbell. "You too. Get out of my way." He shoves her as he passes. She loses her balance and catches herself on Carlos's desk. A couple more kids start crying.

"Hey, hey," I yell at Stutts. My muscles are tensed and primed to fight him, but I don't dare move. "You didn't have to do that."

"Shut up," he shouts at me.

"I'm okay, I'm fine," Mrs. Campbell says, pushing herself back up quickly.

Stutts storms over to Patrick's desk, waving the gun too damn close to the kids' heads as he passes. DeQuan's eyes are huge, and Tyler actually ducks. Stutts grabs his son's arm and yanks him out of his seat. Patrick reaches behind him for his backpack.

"Leave it," Stutts orders as he pulls Patrick up the aisle toward the door. He shoves the gun back into his pocket, then they disappear down the hallway. Mrs. Campbell moves to follow them, but I step forward to stop her.

"I'll go, Mrs. C. You stay with these guys." She looks at me, obviously torn between helping Patrick and looking after the others. "Don't worry; he's not going to hurt his own kid." I'm not sure I believe it, but it sounds good, and she pauses.

I feel a tug at my pants leg, and Simon is there. I never even saw him slip out of his seat. "Stay with *us*, Gus," he says, looking up at me, his dead-serious eyes huge behind thick glass.

It's a rhyming game Simon and I started the first week we were here. Mrs. C. asked Emery and me to help with Reading Circle, and I wound up reading a book to them about Simple Simon who met a pieman. I started calling him Simon the Pieman, and he called me Jakeman the Cakeman, and it kept going from there.

Simon grips my leg like a spider monkey so I can't go out in the hall; I reach down and put my hand on his head. "Have no fear, Cakeman's here. I'll be right back, buddy. I promise."

He looks up at me without blinking, then lets go.

Mrs. Campbell gives me a go-ahead nod, and I move toward the door.

And then—Stutts is back, pushing a white-faced Patrick in front of him.

"Damn security guard's out there. Do those guys carry weapons?" he asks.

"I don't know, Mr. Stutts. Why don't you just leave Patrick for now?" Mrs. C. tries again. "I'm sure we can work something out."

"Yeah, well, you obviously don't know my wife. She's not really into 'working things out' these days. I'm taking my boy—soon as that guy leaves." He glares at the kids. "Everybody sit down." He jerks his head toward two medium-size chairs near the wall. "You two sit there," he tells Emery and Mrs. Campbell. Emery sits down, keeping her eyes on Stutts. She reaches up to twirl a piece of her hair; it's what she does when she's nervous or upset. Mrs. Campbell scoots her chair closer to the kids before she sits in it.

I walk to the back and sit on top of a table. Stutts stands near the door. He leaves the gun in his pocket, but we all know it's there.

"You," he says to me, "close those blinds back there." I move to lower the blinds, keeping a lookout for anyone I can try to signal, but there are no signs of life.

"The rest of you go on with what you were doing," he barks at us. "I don't want anybody staring at me. I gotta think a minute."

Mrs. Campbell takes a deep breath and smiles at the kids. "I have a word search puzzle I saved for free time. Why don't we give our French teachers a break for now?"

Good thinking, Mrs. C. I wasn't big on performing in front of G.I. Joe.

She gets the papers from the tray on her desk and starts handing them out. "Let's see who can be first to find all the words that have to do with fall," she says, all chipper like there's not a crazy guy with a gun watching us. "They're listed on the bottom of the page. Use your sight skills to match them up."

Emery leans over to help Carlos. Her straight hair—dark blond with leftover streaks from summer—swings across her face as she looks down to point to a word.

Emery always looks great, but she's not obsessed with her looks. I've never seen her pull out a mirror in class or mess with her hair. Her eyelashes are long and dark, and she doesn't wear tons of makeup or talk about her new shoes or her damn Louie Whoever bag like a lot of girls do. It's like she knows what's important and what's not. I know she's got some physical stuff going on—she told me about her dizzy spells—but seriously, that girl's steady as a rock.

The kids are already working like crazy. Alicia has her tongue out, and Kenji's studying the puzzle like it's the freakin' Declaration of Independence. It's like their little heads are gonna explode if they don't have something else to focus on.

I can relate. I'm wishing like hell I had some kind of plan.

I can't . . . I can't think straight. It's like that kid Ralph in *Lord of the Flies*. Every time he tries to figure out what to do, a curtain comes down in his head. My English teacher said it's because he's too young to know how to organize a whole colony of boys into a civilized society. He's basically on overload, so his brain kinda short-circuits. I didn't get what she was saying back then, but I do now. I wish these kids had somebody besides a total screwup like me to help them. I used to think of myself as one of the good guys, but after treating Emery like crap and getting hauled down to the jail, I'm not so sure anymore. Maybe the evil stepmother is right about me.

"The Christine" definitely doesn't think much of me. The last time I got in-house suspension, she told me I'm gonna grow up to be a juvenile delinquent. But how can you *grow up* to be a *juvenile* anything? And it was a cell phone infraction—not exactly a capital offense. I swear, you can't fart in our school without getting in-house suspension.

The Christine butts into every conversation I try to have with my dad. Since they've been together, it's like he doesn't hear me anymore. The night he picked me up at the police station, I tried to tell him it wasn't my weed and I hadn't been smoking. It was clear he didn't believe me at first—and then he went off on me for not telling the cops it was Cole's.

I was so sure Cole would tell them it was his. I get it that you're assumed to be guilty if you're caught with somebody who's smoking; my dad's warned me about that. But I also knew from other kids' experiences that I'd have a good chance of getting off if Cole owned up and told the truth. I kept looking at him in the car on the way to the station, but he just looked away. The cop even asked us after he brought us in if anybody had anything else to say, so it wasn't like Cole didn't have every opportunity to speak up. I was pretty shocked when he didn't and all three of us were charged.

I asked him the next day why he let me take the heat, too, but he didn't answer. I was so mad, I didn't speak to him for a couple of weeks—but eventually I let it go. Maybe I did deserve to be punished, too; I could have made him put it away that night, but I didn't.

The only thing I can figure is, Cole's dad's pretty rough on him, so he might have thought he'd get beat worse if he said it was his. I've seen marks on his legs that look like he was hit with a belt, but he won't talk about that, either.

It's hard to stay mad at Cole. He's more like family to me than my own family. Since my brother, Stephen, left for college, Cole is the one who's got my back.

When my mom died and my dad had to go away on business a week later, Cole sat with me for days, watching TV while I drank myself into a stupor. He didn't say ten words, but he stayed right there with me. Finally he took the whiskey bottle away and said, "Let's get you some food, Willoughby."

I wish Emery could get past Cole's badass image; honestly, he just keeps that going for fun. They'd get along great if they weren't so busy judging each other. I mean, I made an effort to get along with her friends. Molly's pretty easy to like, but Tab is moody as hell. And she hates Cole 'cause he calls her STD. Man, what were her parents thinking when they named her Sarah Tabitha? Didn't they remember their last name was Deason?

Stutts keeps looking out the door, and Patrick is standing next to him, eyes on the floor. Hell, I can't stand seeing that kid up there all by himself. I pick up a word search puzzle and pencil, grab his backpack off his chair, walk to the front, and hand them to him. Then I pull out a chair for him at the learning center table nearby. He glances nervously at his dad, but Stutts ignores him, so Patrick takes a seat and looks at the page in front of him.

I lean down and show him the word *pumpkin* in the grid and in the word bank below the puzzle. Patrick circles it, and I squeeze his shoulder. He looks up at me and actually smiles a little.

In a sudden move that catches both of us off guard, Stutts lunges across the table, rips the puzzle out of Patrick's hands, crumples it up in his fist, and throws it on the floor. "I *said* don't tell my boy what to do," he growls at me.

I stare back at him. I want to hit him so bad it hurts. Emery looks up in shock at Stutts's cruelty.

Alicia interrupts the moment, keeping me from saying something I shouldn't. "Mrs. Campbell, hey, Mrs. Campbell." She's waving her hand like mad in the back of the room. "You said we could go outside for a nature walk today. Can we still go?"

"Honey, let's do that tomorrow," Mrs. C. answers.

"My grandpa, he fell and broke his big toe," Olivia announces loudly to no one in particular, "and the doctor says they might cut it off because he's got Die-BB's."

Okay, maybe the kids don't completely understand. Just when you think they must be terrified, one of them says something off-the-wall. And maybe it's a good thing that they're kind of clueless.

"I'm sorry about your grandpa, Olivia," Mrs. C. says. "Now let's do our work quietly, okay, everyone?"

I force myself to calm down and try a different tactic— my legendary charm—on Stutts.

"Hey, man, why don't you let me walk down the hall and check it out for you?" I say. "I can see where the security guy is and—"

"Yeah, right, buddy, you're not goin' anywhere," Stutts interrupts.

"I'm in your camp, sir. You oughta be able to take your kid home from school; that's what I think. I'm just trying to help you." That part's the truth. I really don't think he'd hurt Patrick, and I figure if we can get this maniac away from the other kids, we can deal with the Patrick situation later. It seems to me like a little cooperation could save a lot of kids today.

"Nobody leaves this room," he snaps.

I walk away without commenting. My eyes drift up to a *Kung Fu Panda* poster near the door that says WISE TURTLE SAYS, "YESTERDAY IS HISTORY. TOMORROW IS A MYSTERY. BUT TODAY

IS A GIFT. THAT IS WHY IT IS CALLED THE PRESENT." I'm not sure the first graders get that, but I'm feelin' it right now. I'm definitely focused on the here and now—and I hope to hell my sorry ass'll still be here tomorrow. Now that I'm faced with the possibility of death, it seems kind of important to try to make up for some of my past mistakes. But that'll be kinda hard if I have no future.

CHAPTER 5

Emery

I watch the hallway through the open door while I help Natalie with the word search. Stutts is watching, too. He flexes his shoulders, and when he stretches his neck, the tattooed lizard claws give me the creeps. Had Mrs. Campbell met Patrick's dad before? Did she know he was unstable?

"Great job, cutie-pie!" I say to Janita, who holds up her paper from across the aisle. She beams at me.

"Am I a cutie-pie, too?" Natalie asks, pouting.

"Most definitely," I tell her, and she nods happily.

A kid in a navy blue jacket walks past the door but doesn't look in. He's the only person I've seen go past.

I slide my cell phone out of my pocket, barely moving. Simon cuts his eyes over at me, and I shake my head at him to keep quiet. I'm holding it under the desktop, deciding who to text for help, when Stutts looks up. There's no way he saw me—I was really careful—but he apparently had the same idea at the same time I did.

"Alla you kids put your hands on top of the tables where I can see 'em." Thirty-six little hands flatten on top of the desks. "How many of you've got cell phones?"

Alicia's and Nick's hands go up. I look at Jake and he raises his. I raise mine reluctantly. Lying to a man with a gun in a room full of children seems like a bad idea. The kids look petrified, and I barely have time to think about how weird it is that first graders have cell phones.

"Hand 'em over. Nobody's calling mommy." He collects the phones and dumps them onto the table where Patrick's sitting. "Where's yours, Teach?" He turns to Mrs. Campbell.

"My phone is broken," she says evenly. "I dropped it yesterday."

"You better not be lying to me."

"Mr. Stutts, would you like to search my bag?"

She reaches under her desk for her purse and holds it out to him, looking him calmly in the eye. He drops his eyes first.

"Forget it," he mumbles.

Alicia's waving her hand in the back of the room again.

"Yes, Alicia?" Mrs. Campbell asks.

"Mrs. Campbell, I can't find *tree* anywhere on here."

"Just skip to one of the others, Alicia. You don't have to

do them in order." It's the first time I've heard her sound impatient—ever.

Kenji erases and erases, hard enough to tear a hole in the paper. Lewis slides out of his seat and begins crawling on the floor toward the fish tank again, but Jake stops him and sends him back. The buzz of a leaf blower drifts across the room, an undercurrent to the hum of the minifridge in the back. It seems odd for birds to sing and butterflies to float past when eighteen children are being held at gunpoint by a lunatic.

I feel paralyzed and helpless. Tab says I'm not good at making decisions because my mom's always made them for me. Mom's the queen of passive-aggressive parenting. Her favorite is the rhetorical question: "Is that what you're wearing today?" she'll ask me on my way out the door to school. It's hard to move forward when someone second-guesses everything you do. She always wants to know everything about every aspect of my life, and she loves to call my friends' moms to share gossip. She had plenty to say about my relationship with Jake. She liked him at first—but she made it clear she didn't think it would last.

"Doesn't it bother you the way he flirts with other girls?" she asked after telling me she saw him at the mall talking with Callie Edwards. She knew very well they used to go out. She watched my reaction like a cat playing with a mouse. I've only recently been able to admit to myself that mean might be her natural disposition; it's almost like hurting other people somehow evens the score for the times she's been hurt. I love her; she's my mom. But sometimes I don't like her.

"That's just Jake, Mom. He's friendly to everybody." I wouldn't give her the satisfaction of knowing she got to me. "And Callie works there." Of course, I immediately called Molly in a panic to see if she'd heard anything about Jake hooking up with Callie again; she hadn't. My mother loves mind games, and she can sniff out your weak spot like a drug dog.

I used to believe all the things she said about my dad. She made me think he didn't love us and didn't want to be with us. Only recently, I've realized that maybe he left because she tried to control him, too. I called him once last year when I started figuring things out, but she caught me and didn't speak to me for a week. And it was really awkward talking to him when we've lost so many years. She's made it so difficult for us to have any kind of relationship. Sometimes I feel like all I'll ever have is a few fuzzy memories.

Dancing with my feet on his shoes.

Being lifted up in his strong arms in my pajamas to watch the Fourth of July fireworks.

Wearing the mittens he made from socks so I wouldn't scratch my chicken pox.

And sometimes when he'd come home from work really late, he'd wake me up and we'd sneak into the kitchen and eat ice cream. He always made me promise not to tell Mom, but he said he was missing me and wanted to see me. We'd giggle while we washed the bowls to hide the evidence, and then we'd tiptoe back to bed.

I've saved the images of my father like pretty shells collected on the beach. I keep them mostly locked away, but every now and then, late at night, I take them out. They always make me cry.

Sometimes I wonder if I'll be bad at relationships, too.

Simon raises his hand and catches my eye. I stand up to go help him, and I feel my blood pressure shoot up. My head feels light and my hands are shaking. I can't let the kids see I'm having trouble. I have to hold it together for them.

Before I was diagnosed with POTS, before I knew what postural orthostatic tachycardia syndrome was, I didn't know what was happening to me. When I started high school, I had these spells where I was sure I was having a heart attack. I'd go to stand up and my vision would dim, my heart would race, and I'd fight to keep from passing out. After it passed, I was always drained and exhausted.

Mom thought it was some kind of teenage hypochondria, but by tenth grade things were worse, so she started taking me to doctors. At first no one could find anything wrong, and after trips to three different doctors, even I was starting to think maybe it really was all in my head.

Finally, thank God, Dr. Blackwood diagnosed me with

POTS. It turns out one in a hundred teens have postural orthostatic tachycardia syndrome, but most doctors have never heard of it. It's this malfunction in your autonomic system—the system that controls involuntary stuff like breathing and heartbeat. What happens is that sometimes when I stand up, instead of my heart rate speeding up just a little to adjust to the change in gravity, it goes all haywire and shoots up to 130 beats per minute. So I get light-headed and have to sit back down. Some people faint, but I've always been able to ride it out, although it makes me feel awful when it happens.

When Dr. Blackwood showed me how my blood pressure spiked when I stood up, I cried—because I was so happy to finally know what was wrong with me. I knew I could deal with it if I just knew what it was.

Doctors don't know what causes POTS. Some people get it after an illness like mono or some trauma like a car wreck, but I hadn't had either. Since so many high schoolers get it, some doctors think it could be from growing a lot in a short time.

POTS is complicated, so I don't tell many people about it. It's worse in the mornings when I get out of bed and at night if I stand up too fast from lying on the couch. At school I'm able to hide it, probably because I'm sitting instead of lying down so it's not as severe when I stand up.

I told Molly because I tell Molly everything; she's always so sweet and understanding. I wound up having to tell Tab because she got all mad when I didn't want to hang out because I was tired. With POTS, it's like you're running in place all the time, so you're worn out sometimes just from taking a shower or walking to your car after school. Tab acted like she understood, but then she still got all bent out of shape anytime I wouldn't do something with her.

I didn't tell Jake when we first started going out; I hated how it made me feel like some kind of Southern belle stereotype, feeling faint all the time. When I did get up the nerve to tell him, he wanted to know everything about it, and I noticed he was careful not to keep me talking on the phone so late after he knew.

The good news is, for most people POTS goes away after a few years. And it's pretty easy to treat with meds. I take beta-blockers, drink a lot of water, and get eight hours of sleep every night—well, most nights—and I have way less trouble than I used to. Up till now.

The worst part is that anxiety is a trigger. Dr. Blackwood said to try to keep a slow pace and avoid stress.

Um, right . . .

Stutts, who is definitely raising my stress level, watches the kids, then walks to look out into the hallway, his hand in his pocket on the gun.

"Patrick, you be ready when I tell you, you hear me?" Stutts says. Patrick nods. "What are you looking at?" he yells at Jake, making all of us jump practically out of our skin.

Jake holds both hands up. I can tell he's fighting to stay calm. "Nothin', man."

"Alla you, quit staring at me," he snarls at the kids.

Dear God, I'm thinking, *they're just babies. And they're scared. And how can they* not *look at him when he's holding a gun and taking their friend away?* If he didn't want people to look at him, he shouldn't have gone stark raving mad in front of eighteen kids.

The kids pretend to be absorbed in their work—except for Alicia, who really is, her head bent low over her paper, one of her yellow butterfly barrettes coming loose. I walk over and reposition it, careful not to look at Stutts.

"There you go, buttercup," I whisper. "That's better." She rewards me with a half smile.

"I love the way you're working so quietly," Mrs. Campbell says to the kids. She has this great way of turning criticism into positive statements. Instead of *You didn't raise your hand,* she'll say, "I like to listen to people who raise their hands." Instead of *Clean off your desk,* it's "Everyone with a clean desk can line up for our bathroom break."

She does such fun stuff with them, it makes me wish we could stay all day. One morning the whole room smelled like shaving cream because the kids had squirted it on their desks to write down sight words. Kids are hardly ever absent in Mrs. Campbell's class because they know they'll miss something good.

They respond to her now as she circulates among them, straightening Natalie's sweater and smoothing down

Simon's bed-head hair. Her touch is magic; they seem to have forgotten there's a crazy man in the room. I watch her, without any clue that within just a few minutes these kids' lives will be in our hands—after Jake carries the limp body of their teacher out of the room . . .

CHAPTER 6

JAKE

I GLANCE UP AT THE CLOCK: 9:20. IT clicks randomly—not a noise you'd notice unless there's an asshole with a gun in the room to keep things quiet.

"Mrs. Campbell," Kenji calls out from the back of the room. Everybody turns around to look at him. "I have to go to the bathroom," he says, a look of panic on his face.

"Sweetheart, you'll have to wait," Mrs. Campbell says. "Can you hang on for just a little while?"

He nods and looks back down at his book. After about ten seconds, he yells out, "I can't wait. I have to go now."

Mrs. Campbell looks over at Stutts, who glares at Kenji. Then he looks at me.

"You. You take the kid to the bathroom, and don't try to pull anything cute." His eyes go squinty, and he adds, "You don't wanna make me mad."

No sir, we do not.

I tell him, "No problem, I got this." I motion for Kenji, and he's at my side in a flash.

"You got two minutes," Stutts says.

"Two minutes? Um, I don't know how long this is gonna take. Kenji"—I lean down to him and lower my voice—"is this a pee trip or a poop trip, buddy?"

"I gotta pee," he whispers.

"Okay, that's good." I turn back to Stutts. "Listen, stay cool, man. I'll get him back here as quick as I can."

"You don't talk to anybody in the hall. I can see you from right here."

"Got it. C'mon, sport," I say, but Kenji's already out the door.

I usher him down the hall, trying to go slow so I can see if there's any way to get help, but he's doing a pretty desperate pee-pee dance, so we pick up speed. I feel Stutts's eyes on my back.

Kenji reaches up to take my hand. I've learned that first graders are very affectionate—and right now, we could all use a hand to hold.

There's nobody in the hall to even try to signal, and all the other classroom doors are closed. I move my eyes around searching for a security camera. Shit, no luck. I'm not sure there's anything I could do, anyway, with Stutts staring a hole in my back. Does anyone even monitor those things during the day?

As soon as I open the bathroom door, Kenji runs into a stall and slams the door shut. I slump against the wall and look at my face in the mirror. Sweat beads dot my forehead and my eyes have a deer-in-headlights look. I reach for the faucet and splash cold water on my face.

"Kenji, you okay, buddy?" I ask.

"Yep" is the answer, accompanied by a steady stream of water on water.

I notice that the stall door next to Kenji's is closed. "Hey, is somebody in there?"

Dead silence, then a small voice. "Yes."

"Hey, can you open the door? I need help." Crap, I sound like a perv; now the kid'll never come out. "Listen, I'm a teacher. It's okay. You can come out."

The door opens slowly; big brown eyes look up at me from a small face.

"Hey, pal, what's your name?"

"Sebastian."

"Listen, Sebastian. I'm Jake; I'm a student tutor in Mrs. Campbell's class, and she, Mrs. Campbell, needs you to do something for her. It's very, very important, okay? You know Mrs. Campbell?"

He nods. "Uh-huh, I had her last year."

"Great. She needs you to take a message to the front office. Can you do that?"

"Mrs. Boyd said to come right back."

"I know, buddy. But she'll be okay with this. I promise I'll fix it with your teacher."

Sebastian gazes at me, expressionless.

"It'll only take a minute. But listen"— I'm thinking fast—

"after I tell you the message, you have to count to twenty before you leave here to go to the office, okay?" I don't want to scare him, but I need to make him understand the danger. "There's a man in the hall who might see you if you leave right away—and we don't want that. So you're gonna count to twenty first—can you do that before you leave the bathroom?" He nods, so I continue. "And then go down to the office and here's what you tell them: Tell them that there's a man . . . there's a man with a gun in Mrs. Campbell's room."

Big eyes go wide.

"Can you remember that?"

"Is he a bad man?" he asks.

"Well, kind of. Okay, yes, he is, and that's why we need help."

Sebastian turns his back on me abruptly and heads back into the stall.

"Sebastian, hey, where're you going?"

He tries to pull the door shut, but I'm holding it. "They told us if anybody bad comes in the hall while we're in the bathroom, we're supposed to sit on the toilet with our feet up so nobody can see us."

Aw, man, that's about the saddest thing I've ever heard. Kinda makes me sick thinking about a little kid in the toilet with his feet up, all by himself and scared out of his mind. For the first time today, I actually feel like crying.

"Hey, Sebastian, listen, it'll be okay. The bad man's in the classroom, and I'll make sure he stays there."

Sebastian reemerges from the stall and studies me, considering. I'm running out of time before I have to get back.

"You like Mrs. Campbell, right?" I'm guessing everybody likes Mrs. Campbell. Sebastian nods. "Do it for Mrs. Campbell, okay?" I use my most persuasive voice. "She needs you."

The toilet flushes and Kenji comes out. He moves to the sink and turns the water on.

"The bad man's not gonna see me?" Sebastian looks over at Kenji, who's washing his hands like a madman—completely focused on foamy soap and serious rubbing. I can just see him singing that damn happy birthday song over and over in his head like they tell them to do when they're washing their hands, so it's long enough to get the germs off. It's like he's trying to wash the morning off, too.

"No, dude, I'm gonna talk to him so he doesn't see you leave."

Dude looks back at me.

"You got it, little buddy? You can do this. You da man."

He nods again.

"Listen, we have to go back now. Remember, count to twenty—then go to the office and tell them we need help." It seems like a good time to beat a dead horse; this kid's got to get it right. "Which teacher did I tell you?"

"Mrs. Campbell."

"Good. It's up to you, little man. I don't have any other way to let them know we're in trouble." I smile and he looks at me and nods once. "Okay, Kenji, let's go."

Kenji says quietly, "Can I go to the office, too?"

A tear slides down his cheek.

I kneel down beside Kenji and give him my full attention. Some things can't be rushed.

"I wish you could, Kenji, but you heard the man. I think we both have to go back."

Another tear rolls, and he drops his head.

I put my hand on his shoulder. "I'm not going to let anything happen to you. I promise. Look at me."

He looks up.

"Everything's gonna be okay. The school has all kinds of people who can help us, and they're going to come take care of this. And until they get there, you can count on me. Okay?"

Kenji nods, stone-faced.

"Listen, tell me who's better—Superman or Batman."

"Batman," he says definitively.

"Well, then, I'm gonna be Batman and you're gonna be Robin, and nobody can hurt the Daring Duo, right?"

He shakes his head, lips pressed together.

"What?"

"I want to be Batman."

"Okay, cool. You be Batman and I'll be Robin."

I reach out my hand, and he locks on me with a death grip as I stand up, and we walk back out the door. He glances down the hall at Stutts waiting for us and turns back to the water fountain. I need to clear him out of here fast so Sebastian can leave, but I can't blame him for wanting to put off the inevitable, so I give him a boost. "Real quick, okay?"

He drinks like his head's on fire, but I stop him after a few seconds.

"Come on, Batman," I tell him. "We gotta get back to the cave."

I scoop him up and carry him in a football hold so I can move him quickly down the hall. He yells at first, then giggles.

Still no doors open. Still no people in the hallway.

Come on, Sebastian, get it right. I speed up some more.

I step back into the room and set Kenji upright.

Stutts watches me suspiciously from the doorway, then glances down at the bathroom. "Was anybody in there?"

"Nope, just me and Kenji. Batman and Robin." Kenji gives me a look. "I mean Robin and Batman."

Stutts eyes both of us, then reenters the room. "No more bathroom trips," he says. "Patrick, you be ready. When the hall's clear, we're going."

Patrick nods, head tucked.

"Thank you, Jake," Mrs. Campbell says.

"No problem," I tell her, and she smiles.

I feel a tug on my pants leg and Simon's there again. How does he do that? I never see him coming. "You came back, Jack," he says seriously. Before I can answer him, Stutts is yelling orders at us again.

"All right, everybody stay put. I'm just gonna take another look out there."

He turns toward the hall—just about the time Sebastian will be leaving!

"Mr. Stutts," I call out, frantically thinking of a way to stall for time.

"What do you want?" He stops and looks back at me.

"I, um, I have an idea." *Damn, I wish I had an idea.*

"Spit it out, kid. I don't have all day."

"Listen, what if we called your wife to come down here and straighten all this out? We can all have a big meeting and try to—"

"I don't need your help, kid. And I don't want her here. She's trying to take me to court to keep me from seeing my boy."

"I'm sure she'll listen to—" I'm just babbling now, and Emery's frowning at me.

"She changed the locks!" he yells. "On my own damn house! She won't listen to anybody, except her mother, and that woman's hated me from the first day I met her. She never thought I was good enough for her precious daughter, and she poisoned her against me."

"There must be someone else who can help you with—" I start out, but he cuts me off.

"That's enough," Stutts says. "It's none of your business. Now, everybody stay right where you are. Nobody moves."

I hold my breath while he steps out into the hall, his hand on the gun in the pocket of his pants.

"What are you *doing?*" Emery whispers.

"I'll explain later," I tell her.

And then he's back. Sebastian must have made it out,

thank God. "Hey, Teach, do they have any kinda schedule—those guards?" he asks.

"Not really. They move around during the day to different halls."

There's a long silence.

"Mr. Stutts, I'm sure you're not the kind of man who—" Mrs. Campbell starts.

"You don't *know* what kind of man I am!" he yells in a sudden rage, slamming his fist against the door, making everyone jump again. "You don't know *anything* about me! I'm not the kind of man to kill people? Is that what you were gonna say? That's not what the US Army says. They think I'm exactly that kind of man!" He steps toward her, his finger stabbing the air as he yells. "They trained me to kill and sent me to Iraq to do it. They give medals for it, did you know that?" His face is red. "You gonna argue with the US government, Teacher Lady? You think you know more than Uncle Sam? They'll tell you what kind of man I am."

He stops, and I hear sniffles from the back of the room.

"I'm sure you discharged your duties as a soldier admirably." Mrs. Campbell speaks softly, looking him right in the eye. "I didn't realize you're a war hero."

"Don't say that word to me!" Stutts shouts. He steps close, towering over her, but Willa Campbell doesn't blink. "I'm no hero," he yells. "The heroes are the ones who didn't come home. Don't you throw that word around, 'cause you've got *no* idea what it means." He's breathing heavy and it's hard to believe no one's heard him out in the hall.

Emery comforts Rose, who's crying softly. "Shh, it's okay, pumpkin."

"I'm sorry, Mr. Stutts," Mrs. Campbell says. "I was only trying to honor the sacrifices you've made to protect people like me."

He glares at her. Then his hostile posture deflates a little. After a couple of seconds, he turns away and mumbles, almost to himself, "I was just doing my duty, that's all."

"He said *doodie*," Mason stage-whispers. I glare at him and he shuts up.

CHAPTER 7

Emery

Stutts's screaming has scared the kids half to death, and my knees are shaking again. I don't know how Mrs. Campbell stands up to him when he's like that. Jake's jaw is locked, and I can tell he's gritting his teeth.

We're all barely breathing and the tension in the room is thick.

Then—a sudden movement in the doorway causes all of us to look up. I only have a second to register a man there. The security guy. The short, baby-faced one who's always on his cell phone. He's standing in the doorway with one hand on his hip and one hand on the door frame, just looking in like he's about to say something.

What is he thinking? Does he know Stutts is armed? His face doesn't show any alarm.

Before anyone can say a word, and before the guard has a chance to speak, the unthinkable happens.

It happens so fast, I'm not even sure of what I'm seeing—until it's over.

Stutts swings his entire body toward the door and raises his arm, all in one motion.

A huge explosion rocks the room.

The security guard grabs his chest and staggers backward, no longer in sight in the doorway.

Stutts's stance is wide, knees bent, body tensed, his arm outstretched as the echo of the horrendous boom rings through the classroom. There's a high-pitched tone in my ears and the children's screams sound far away. We all look from the gun in his hand to the empty doorway, afraid to move.

"Everybody, get down," Mrs. Campbell yells, and five or six kids immediately slide from their chairs and cower on the floor. As soon as the rest of the kids understand, they hit the floor, too. I slide from my chair and crouch down, hovering over the kids nearest me, spreading my arms out to protect them, knowing it won't be nearly enough if he starts shooting into the classroom.

"Keep your heads down," I tell them, my voice shaking.

Oh God, oh God, I think he might have killed him! He shot the security guard! My head feels like it's going to explode. The room goes white and I struggle to hang on to consciousness.

I look over at Jake, who's also placed himself between Stutts and the kids on his side of the room. Mrs. Campbell kneels between Stutts and the children near her, shielding them. She has her back to Stutts, totally focused on the kids.

"I told you I'd shoot!" Stutts is yelling, his voice shaking and panicked. "You saw him. He was going for his gun." He's pale and sweaty and gasping for breath. He grabs his chest with his free hand and staggers backward. He's lost it! If he's having a full-blown panic attack, anything can happen.

Several of the kids cling to me. *Please, God, don't let him hurt them.*

"You don't—confront—a soldier!" Stutts is screaming, his breath coming in short spurts. "You saw him," he shouts at us. "He was going for his gun. Somebody threatens me— I'm gonna shoot back!"

Beyond his yelling, I'm aware of people running and shouting in the hallway. A door slams, and suddenly the intercom clicks on.

"Code Red. Teachers, lock your doors and keep your students inside the classrooms." The principal's voice is loud and urgent. "We are under an emergency alert. Teachers, do *not* allow students to leave your classroom for *any* reason. Lock your doors and keep your students *inside*." He pauses, then says more slowly, "Teachers, this is *not* a drill!"

And then an eerie quiet falls. The lines from a poem float through my brain: "Things fall apart; the centre cannot hold; The blood-dimmed tide is loosed, and everywhere The ceremony of innocence is drowned . . ." W. B. Yeats. "The

Second Coming." I had to memorize it last year, but I had no idea it was still there in my head. I wonder what innocence these kids will have left.

Stutts is watching the door and pacing back and forth like a caged animal. I can see the gun in his hand shaking.

The room goes fuzzy and I blink to clear my vision. I pick out a poster on the wall and stare—THE SILENT E. A magician in a tall pointed hat changes words with his wand: *cap* becomes *cape; hop* becomes *hope.* Hope. I repeat the word over and over as I try to breathe deeply and slowly.

And then I see poor Patrick—still in the chair in the front of the room, hunched over, hugging his knees. I want to go to him, but I know I can't. It breaks my heart to see him there alone.

Stutts grabs his son roughly. "C'mon, kid. We're gettin' out of here."

Patrick's eyes flash his terror as he's yanked by his arm toward the door.

Stutts leans his head out and looks down the hall. He immediately pulls back into the classroom. "Shit! You tell them to clear that hall," he yells at Mrs. Campbell. "I don't want to see anybody looking around that corner. You tell them—if they don't let me leave with my boy, somebody's gonna get hurt!"

He doesn't even seem to realize somebody already has.

Mrs. Campbell stands up and walks slowly toward him, speaking in a soothing voice. "Mr. Stutts, I don't have any access to speak to them." She looks over at the remains of the telephone. "Just let me go out and talk to the people in the hall about what we need to do."

"You're not goin' out there. You're not gonna bring them in here. You just want to tell them to rush me."

He looks crazed, out of control. *Armed and dangerous*— I suddenly understand what it means.

"You're in charge here, Mr. Stutts," she says, her hands held up in a gesture of total surrender. "I'll do whatever you want."

Several students are crying. "I think I'm gonna puke," Natalie announces, and I look around frantically for the trash can. DeQuan reaches for an empty plastic bin on a table near him and passes it to her. Natalie bends over it, gagging, but nothing comes up.

"Shut up and let me think. Everybody stay where you are," Stutts yells at the kids, glancing away from the door for only a second. "Nobody move unless I say so."

He's pacing, prowling, and fidgeting with the gun, both hands on it now. "I gotta think what to do," he mutters to himself.

He looks up at the sound of a siren in the distance, growing louder as it gets closer. The noise stops abruptly on the street in front of the school.

Suddenly the intercom crackles again. "Mrs. Campbell, is everyone all right in there?" I'm sure even the kids can hear the effort the principal's making to sound normal.

Mrs. Campbell looks at Stutts for permission to answer, but he ignores her. "We're okay," she says.

"Is anyone hurt?" the tense voice asks.

"No, no one's hurt." She pauses. "Not in the room."

Poor security guy. He was definitely hurt, but we don't know how badly.

She continues, "Mr. Stutts will not harm the children." Good move, Mrs. C. She let them know his name and used her self-fulfilling prophecy trick at the same time.

"Quiet!" Stutts cuts her off. "I'll do the talking here."

"Mr. Stutts, please do not hurt anyone," the intercom continues. "We'll do whatever we can to resolve this situation peacefully. Just give us a chance to talk to you about what you want."

I try to remember the principal's name; Mrs. Campbell always refers to him as "the Big Cheese." If she has to go down to the office, she winks at the children and tells them the Big Cheese needs to see her. I haven't figured out if she likes him or not.

"What I *want* is to take my son out of here," Stutts yells, jabbing his finger at the intercom as if the principal can see him.

"Mr. Stutts, let me come down there, and I'll bring you back here to the office where we can talk."

"I'm *done* with talking. You've been talking to my wife. You're all on *her* side. You just want to keep me from my son."

"Mr. Stutts, why don't we—"

"That's enough," he yells. "Turn that thing off."

I hold my breath and, thankfully, the intercom clicks off.

Mrs. Campbell's face is chalky and I notice sweat beading her upper lip, but she manages to swing into teacher mode.

"Class, everyone needs to move to the reading carpet in the back. We can finish the coloring puzzles we started yesterday," she says. "I'll put the crayon boxes on the floor."

A couple of *yays* and several relieved smiles. They liked the coloring puzzle.

"But we can't color on the carpet," Kimberly says.

"We'll pass out books for you to hold in your laps," Mrs. Campbell tells them, and I realize she's moving them to the floor to keep their heads low. "Quickly, now." Mrs. Campbell claps her hands at them as they scatter. She reaches for the puzzles from the tray on her desk, and I notice her hand shaking as she holds them out to Jake.

"I'll get out the crayon boxes," I tell her.

Jake hands out the puzzles, and Mrs. Campbell passes out books from the bookcase.

Stutts stands in the doorway, gripping Patrick's arm. As soon as we've passed everything out, the kids start coloring. Jake and I sit on the floor with them. Mrs. Campbell walks back up to her desk. She seems exhausted; I watch her hold on to the desktop to lower herself into her chair.

The big clock in the front of the room makes a noise. It's only 9:45—a little over an hour has passed since Jake and

I got here. We should be leaving now to get back to school. Guess they'll figure out we're not there at some point. My mom will never let me leave the house again after this—if I ever make it home. Oh God, will I make it home?

All of a sudden, Mason yells out Mrs. Campbell's name, and I look up just in time to see her slump from her chair to the floor.

CHAPTER 8
JAKE

I WATCH IN TOTAL SHOCK AS WILLA Campbell's body goes completely limp and she slides from her chair to the floor. *What the hell is happening?* She lands facedown with her arm bent under her head, almost like she's just curled up for a nap. Emery jumps up and runs to her, spilling crayons everywhere, and I race to help—not even thinking about that maniac Stutts for once.

Emery kneels beside her; she reaches down and shakes her shoulder. "Mrs. Campbell. Mrs. Campbell, are you okay?" The teacher's head's twisted at a weird angle to the side. Her hair's covering her face, but it's obvious she's out cold.

"We need to roll her over to see if she's hurt," Emery says, looking up at me.

I reach down and move her as easy as I can. Her face is pale and sweaty, her eyes are closed, and her mouth is open a little.

"Mrs. Campbell," Emery says, close to her face. "Mrs. C., can you hear me?"

The kids are starting to crowd around. I hold up a hand. "Hey, guys, everybody move back so she can get some air."

"Is she dead?" Natalie wails.

Emery looks up in shock. "Oh, honey, no."

"Is she going to be okay?" Rose asks.

"She's gonna be fine," I tell her. "She just fainted, that's all. People do it all the time."

"Jake, can you help me lean her up?" Emery asks.

I move closer and slide my hand under her back. I lift her shoulders and lean her body against me, holding her head to keep it from rolling. It feels weird touching her like this.

"Mrs. Campbell, can you hear me?" Emery asks again, close to her ear.

Stutts seems to come out of a daze. "What's going on? Is she okay?" He walks closer, looking back and forth from her to the door. "Wake her up. You hear me? Wake her up!"

Emery gets very still. She's taking deep breaths and staring at a spot in front of her and squeezing her eyes shut and then opening them. If she has one of those attacks right now, I'm gonna be on my own here.

"Emery, you okay? Don't you go passing out on me, too," I say to her in a low voice.

Emery glances up at me and then I can see she's about to lose it. I'm not sure if she's mad at herself for nearly fainting or at me for noticing. Or Stutts for—well, being Stutts. She hardly ever gets really steamed, but she can go from angel to kick-ass ninja in about three seconds if you really get her riled.

"Mr. Stutts, I'm trying." Emery turns on Stutts, facing him down like a warrior. "We're doing the best we can, so just cut us some slack. And put that gun away before you hurt somebody. This is no time to be waving it around."

Ohhhh crap, this is not a good plan. "Emery, here, we can use this to fan her." I grab a notebook from the teacher's desk, trying to distract her before she really goes off on him. Stutts looks hypnotized; you can tell people don't stand up to him very often. He doesn't put the gun away, but he does hold it more carefully at his side.

"You want my water?" Simon asks, holding a plastic bottle toward us. "Mrs. Campbell can have it."

"Thanks, Simon," Emery says. "Good idea."

"You da man, Tarzan," I say to Simon. "Pour it on this and you can wipe her face with it," I tell Emery, stripping off the long-sleeved button-down I'm wearing over my T-shirt and handing it over. Oh great. The *one* day I wear the freakin' Justin Bieber shirt my grandmother gave me for my birthday. It was all I could find this morning, 'cause my crazy stepmom destroyed all my T-shirts. The Christine went into my room and took scissors and cut out all the slogans she didn't like. And then she put the mutilated shirts back in my drawer! That woman is crazy as an outhouse rat. I put this one on today 'cause I figured it'd be under my other shirt where no one would see it. Simon checks it out, but

Emery doesn't notice as she pours water on the shirt I've handed her.

There's a soft buzzing sound. Stutts reaches onto the desk and holds out a cell phone to me. It's mine. "Turn it off. I don't want to listen to that." I glance down. Dad. Word has reached the mayor's office. I turn it off and hand it back to Stutts.

"This one, too." He hands me another buzzing phone. I switch it off and give it back to him. Looks like the whole town's heard what's going on. As much as I hate to worry everybody, I'm glad they know. Maybe somebody'll figure out what the hell to do.

Emery wipes Mrs. Campbell's face. Then she stops and looks up.

"Hey, does anybody remember seeing Mrs. Campbell giving herself a shot?"

Mason raises his hand. "I saw her. I came in at lunch one day because I forgot my lunch money, and she had a needle sticked in her arm." Mason Mayfield III's very proud of being the keeper of this information; then he looks worried. "She told me not to tell anybody. She said it might scare the other kids."

"Good job, Mason. That's important information," Emery says as she reaches inside Mrs. Campbell's sleeve. "You did the right thing telling us. Jake, look." She turns the medic alert bracelet so I can read it.

Emery looks up at Stutts. "She's diabetic. We've got to get her out of here."

"She has Die-BB's?" Olivia yells, alarmed.

"It's okay, honey. She'll be fine," Emery says.

"This is some kinda trick," Stutts shouts, pacing back and forth. "You just want to let the cops in."

"Mr. Stutts, Mrs. Campbell needs medical attention," Emery tells him.

"Diabetic comas are dangerous." I stand up so I can look him in the eye. I'm almost as tall as he is. "This is serious, man."

Stutts stares back at me. I move closer so I can talk low without the kids hearing.

"Look, she could die. We can't let that happen."

"Don't tell me what to do," he says.

I stare him down because I know that one way or another, I'm *going* to get help for her.

"I'm not letting anybody in here," he says.

"Just let me carry her out, man. I can take her down to the office and they can call the paramedics."

"Jake, can you bring me her purse?" Emery asks. "She keeps it under her desk."

I move to the desk, pick up the purse, and toss it at Emery. "You looking for insulin?"

"Yeah, I guess that's what she needs, but I'm not sure what to do with it if we find any." She digs through the bag. "Nothing here."

"I'll try her desk," I say.

I search quickly, plowing through notepads and rulers and pencils and Band-Aids. Nothing.

"Hey, does it have to be refrigerated?" I ask, moving toward the back of the room.

"I don't know . . . maybe," Emery says.

I open the minifridge. "Nothing but Diet Cokes."

I walk back toward Stutts. Mrs. Campbell needs help, and we're the only ones who can get it for her. "Mr. Stutts, let me carry her to the front office and I'll come right back. I give you my word I won't bring anyone back with me."

Stutts glances at Patrick, like he's looking for an answer, his face blotchy red.

"We may not have much time," I tell him, turning my back to the kids, hoping they don't hear.

He gives me a long look. I stare back. Finally, he says, "Okay. Just you. You come right back. And don't try anything. You hear?"

"No problem," I say, springing into action. Emery helps me lift the teacher as I bend down, slide my arms under her shoulders and knees, and pick her up from the floor. I shift Mrs. C.'s weight onto me and Emery drapes her arm over her body.

"Where are you going?" Natalie asks.

"Jake's going to take her to find a doctor, sweetie," Emery tells her.

"Does she have to have a operation?" Alicia asks.

"No, they're just going to give her the medicine she needs."

"You okay here?" I ask Emery.

She hesitates, then nods. "I'm fine. Go."

"Can we go, too?" Carlos asks.

"Not right now, but maybe in a little bit," Emery tells him. His lip trembles, and she leans down to speak to him; I notice she's leaning on the desk, like she needs the support.

"Emery, you sure you're okay?" The color's gone from her face, and I hate leaving her.

"*Go*, Jake! I'm fine."

She realizes she's snapped at me, and she changes her tone as she reaches out and pulls Carlos to her. "I need you to help me with these coloring puzzles," she says to him. She turns to the other kids. "Will y'all show me what you've done so far?"

The kids flock around her, several talking at once. They love to show off their work. She's herding them to the back of the room as I turn to leave.

I pause at the door, realizing I have no idea what's going on in the hallway. It seems like a good time to give them a heads-up, so I call out, "This is Jake Willoughby. I'm coming out. I'm bringing the teacher, and she's unconscious."

A voice answers, "Come on out, Jake. Nice and slow, okay?" I recognize Reed Walker, the police chief. It hits me they think Stutts might use us as a shield, and I wonder briefly why he doesn't.

I walk through the door and into the hall, lifting my arms a little to shift Mrs. Campbell's limp body toward my chest for better support. It's clear and quiet. All classroom doors are closed. Dark red drops stain the floor—shit—a trail of blood, right where the security guard fell. No sign of his body. A man with a police helmet aims a gun in my direction from around the corner. Chief Walker looks out from behind him.

"Slow and easy, Jake," the chief tells me. "Just keep coming; you're fine." He's watching the hall behind me.

"She's diabetic. She passed out. She needs help!"

I round the corner, and two other police officers crouch low, weapons drawn. A guy with a paramedic badge on his shirt comes from behind them to take Mrs. Campbell while they continue to cover the hall I just came from. Farther down, several men lean over a blueprint of a building, I'm guessing this one, one of them pointing.

What the hell? Are they gonna climb in through the air vents or something? Do they think this is a damn Bruce Willis movie?

After handing off the teacher, my arms feel light but my legs are suddenly tired. Just as I'm about to turn back, a familiar figure steps from the front office.

"Dad." I try to swallow the lump in my throat.

"Jake, are you all right?" he yells as he breaks into a run.

He's racing toward me calling my name, and I run to him like a first grader.

He reaches me and wraps me in a huge bear hug. It's taken me years to catch up to my former linebacker dad's height, and he still has about fifty pounds on me. I've only seen him cry once—the night Mom died—but I feel his chest expand sharply and he says my name in a strangled voice. I hang on to him for a few seconds, then pull away.

"Dad, I have to go back."

"Jake, no! You're not going back in there."

"You have ten seconds," Stutts calls from the classroom. I figure he doesn't want them to have time to ask me questions or give me instructions. "I'm counting," Stutts yells through the hallway. "Ten . . . nine . . . eight . . ."

"Is everybody okay in there?" Chief Walker asks me.

"Yeah, the kids are fine. Scared, but fine." Dad's still holding my arm, but I pull away. "I have to get back or I don't know what he'll do."

". . . seven . . . six . . . five . . ." Stutts yells.

"No one's been hurt?" The chief's holding his walkie-talkie toward me with his thumb on the button, so I know others are listening.

"No, everybody's okay. Don't worry, we'll take care of the kids."

"Who's with you?" he asks.

"Emery. Emery Austin's with me."

"Jake—" Dad starts again.

". . . four . . . three . . ." Stutts counts.

The chief starts to ask me something. "Can you tell me—"

"There's no time. I have to go." I'm already moving back down the hall.

"Jake, be careful, son."

"I will." I stop and look him in the eye so he can see I'm okay. "Dad, don't worry. We'll be okay." Then I sprint toward the classroom.

CHAPTER 9
Emery

As soon as Jake is out of sight, Stutts becomes even more nervous and jittery, like he's afraid he's made a mistake letting him go. He crouches by the door and points the gun down the hall.

It's terrible being in the room without Jake.

Several kids try to talk to me but I shush them, herding them all back to the reading carpet and pointing to their papers. It takes all my energy to fight the rising panic. I even drop a couple of books so I'll have an excuse to lean down to pick them up, a trick I've learned to keep from blacking out. If I can get my head down by pretending to pick something up or get something out of my shoe, it sends the blood flow back to my head without anyone knowing I'm on the verge of passing out.

When Stutts starts the countdown, we're all frozen in fear.

"Ten . . . nine . . . eight . . ."

What will he do if Jake isn't back in time?

"I think I'm gonna puke!" Natalie yells, and I hand her the trash can, barely looking in her direction.

". . . seven . . . six . . . five . . ."

The kids watch the door as Stutts counts.

". . . four . . . three . . ."

I look around the room desperately for something—anything—I can use as a weapon if he starts shooting. How can I stop him if he goes crazy?

". . . two . . . one."

I know this is it. Jake isn't coming back. Stutts will kill us all. How will he decide who to shoot first? Or will he just open fire?

Stutts's flint-hard eyes meet mine. The part of him that's human seems to have shrunk to a tiny pinprick of light. Madness has taken over.

And then—thank you, God—Jake is there.

Tears of relief fill my eyes.

"I'm here. It's okay, guys. And Mrs. Campbell's gonna be just fine. They're taking good care of her," he says, looking around at the anxious faces as he enters the room.

Jake gives me a long look, and I turn away to keep from falling apart. I've spent so much energy learning to live without him, and now all I want to do is run to him. I don't want him to know how much I need him. A devastating wave of longing washes over me.

He leans down to Natalie with her garbage can. "Natalie,

you okay?" He directs the question to her, but his eyes, full of concern, are on me. I lift my head and lock on his gaze. Natalie nods and sniffles and puts the trash can down, crisis over.

Crisis over. The countdown crisis, anyway. I know there will be others. The kids are watching. I square my shoulders and take a deep breath. Jake and I are now the sole authority figures—the only "adults" standing between them and the crazy man with the gun.

Suddenly Stutts is screaming at Jake. "No one leaves this room again. You got that? I don't care what happens. No one's going anywhere."

Jake holds up his hands and nods but doesn't speak. He can see how wild Stutts is right now.

Stutts didn't say—out loud—that he'd shoot us, but we all know that's what the countdown was about. If he doesn't get what he wants . . .

"I want to go home." Natalie starts to cry again. *Me too, Natalie, me too.*

Several others start up. The absence of their teacher has sparked a panic. I try to channel her calm presence, the way she anchored the rest of us and made the situation seem somehow manageable. Miraculously, I feel my body relax a little as I concentrate on adopting her rocksteady demeanor.

"Our teacher's gone," Kimberly wails.

"Are you gonna leave us, too?" Simon asks, speaking louder than usual above the noise.

"No way, Jose," I answer. Simon looks up, surprised that

I've assumed Jake's rhyming role. Jake grins and comes over to stand beside me.

Suddenly I notice what he's wearing. "Nice shirt, Biscuit," I say, giving Justin Bieber an appraising look. I fight the urge to laugh, which seems ridiculous in this setting. I'm afraid that if I start, I'll never stop.

"Don't start with me," Jake warns, one dark eyebrow cocked in my direction, but he's smiling. He walks over to his wet shirt and picks it up off the floor. I recognize it as one of his brother's hand-me-downs; he loves them because they're soft with age. I try not to think about the way the worn shirts felt against my face, with their fresh cotton smell and their hung-over-the-back-of-the-chair wrinkles.

He slides his arms into the damp sleeves and buttons the shirt over the offending photo. "Man, that's embarrassing," he says with a grin.

That's classic Jake. He told me once the thing that's most embarrassing in life is when other people know you're embarrassed. So if you just admit it up front, nobody makes fun of you because everybody knows how it feels.

It's one of the things I liked best about him from the beginning—that he's totally unself-conscious. Lots of people *say* they don't care what other people think, but Jake really doesn't. He's always the first one to get up and dance at a party—crazy dancing that's so bad, it's almost good.

Sometimes he turns the car radio up and sings really loud. He pocket-dialed me once, and when I listened to my voice mail, I could hear him wailin' on "Single Ladies," singing with Beyoncé in this high girlie voice. When I played it back for him, he just laughed, and then he put my phone on speaker and played it for everybody in art class.

For me, Champion Sociophobe of the Universe, he was a good teacher. He peeled away my shyness and taught me not to take myself so seriously. When I confessed to him how nervous I am when I think other people are watching me, he said, "I promise you, the world isn't looking at you. Everybody's too busy. And basically, most people just care about themselves, if you wanna know the truth."

When I admitted I'm paralyzed sometimes by fear of screwing up, he laughed and said, "You know, Em, if you do screw up, people will remember it for about two minutes until they move on to the next person who screws up—well, unless you're Marilyn Holderfield and you wet your pants in fourth grade; people do kinda remember that one."

Jake makes everyone else feel like it's okay to mess up. I'll never forget the day this poor ninth grade girl tripped in the lunchroom and her food went all over her and she slipped and went down in the mess. The whole school was staring at her. People started laughing and pointing. The girl just sat there on the floor, her head down, about to burst out crying.

And then, before she could even try to get back up, Jake was there. He sat down next to her on the floor, like they'd planned a big ole picnic, and started talking to her, telling her jokes and acting like nothing was wrong—he even picked up a cookie off the floor, gave her half, and started eating the other half.

After everybody lost interest in them, he helped the girl up, looped her hand through his arm, and made a big production of escorting her to her table.

Yep, you guessed it. The ninth grade girl was me.

It was the beginning of my heart-stabbing, gut-twisting, butterfly-producing crush on Jake Willoughby.

"I'm hungry," Mason Mayfield III yells at the top of his lungs, bringing my thoughts back to the first graders around me. "When do we eat?"

"Is Mrs. Campbell coming back?" Rose asks.

"No, but don't you worry," Jake tells her. "We'll be just fine, Valentine." He winks at me.

"Quiet!" Stutts barks at them. "I've had about enough of all this racket." But the racket continues.

"There's ants everywhere!" Mason yells. "All over the place." He jumps up and starts stomping the floor around him like he's doing some kind of war dance. Within seconds, all the kids are up and running, jumping across the ants that have appeared out of nowhere and are swirling in wavy lines across the floor.

Lewis immediately begins to howl. "Stop! Don't hurt 'em. They're mine." He shoves Mason to the floor. Mason gets up and makes a dive for Lewis, knocking him down.

The two of them roll over each other on top of the scattering ants, punching and slapping and pulling hair, while the other kids gather around to yell encouragement. Great! Just what we need right now!

"Hey, that's enough!" Jake springs into action, grabbing Mason, so I wade into the fray and pull Lewis off the floor. He's sobbing uncontrollably, trying to drop out of my hold.

"They're my ants. He killed my ants."

"Lewis, stop it," I yell. "Lewis, listen to me. What are you talking about?" I shout above his crying until he finally hears me.

"I found them. They're mine."

"You found them where?"

"Outside."

"You brought them in from outside? When?"

"This morning before school."

"How did you bring them in?"

"In my lunch box."

I look at the trail of ants. It definitely leads to the cubbies in back where the kids' lunches and coats are stored.

"Why would you do that?" I ask.

"Joey Hopper has an ant farm and I didn't never have one."

I let go of Lewis long enough to follow the ant line, which ends at a Spider-Man lunch box. I lift it gingerly by the handle and lay it on the table. When I unlatch the lid and open it, there's a little pile of dirt, several clumps of grass, and an awful lot of ants—who are pretty disturbed about the sudden change of habitat. I slam the lid on the angry insects.

"Oh, Lewis, you shouldn't have done that. Did you get bitten, sweetie?"

He holds up his hand and shows me several small bites on his fingers. "Just a little. But it's okay. They didn't know I was trying to save 'em."

"Where is your lunch?"

"My mom gave me money to buy it. I just brought my lunch box for the ants."

"Get that thing out of here," Stutts growls, impatient with the whole mess. "Get rid of it."

I look up helplessly.

"Throw it out the window," he orders.

"No, no, no." Lewis sets up a howl. "Don't throw my ants out the window!"

"Here." Jake picks up a big plastic storage tub from a shelf and pops the lid off. He dumps some blocks out and throws the lunch box—dirt and grass and all—into the empty bin.

"But what about them ants that got out?" Lewis yells, pointing to the floor.

"We'll get them. Don't worry." I grab a couple of sheets of paper and begin scooping the ants up with them. The irony is not lost on me—that I'm suddenly expending all kinds of energy saving a bunch of ants when a few minutes ago I was worried about children getting killed. You do what you have to do.

I toss the papers into the plastic bin with the rest of the ant paraphernalia.

"But how are they gonna breathe in there?" Lewis whines.

"There's plenty of air inside the bin," Jake tells him with a look that dares him to complain. Lewis takes the hint and pipes down.

Then Mason starts up again. "He hit my lip. He made my teeth hurt."

"There's no blood, Mason. You're fine," I tell him. Several other kids chime in with their versions of the fight.

"These kids are driving me crazy," Stutts yells. I can tell he's about to go ballistic over the noise and chaos.

Suddenly I clap out a rhythm—just like I've heard Mrs. Campbell do. Magically, the kids respond immediately, stopping all noise and clapping back a matching pattern. Mrs. C. does it to keep from yelling over the noise to get their attention, and they love it. Some patterns are simple and others more complex, but she changes them up so they have to listen to repeat them. Several of them look up at me, smiling, and I'm glad I've given them something familiar to hang on to.

"Reading time, everyone," I tell them, changing gears after a few minutes. Their attention spans are so short. "Everyone move back to the reading corner."

"Will you read *Giraffes Can't Dance?*" Janita asks.

"No, read *Strega Nona*," Alicia says.

"Whoever's quietest gets to pick the book," I tell them,

herding them back to the carpeted corner lined with book-shelves. I get them seated and start passing out books. Jake takes one to Patrick. "Everyone can just look at the books for a bit, and then I'll read one to you," I say.

Lewis is lying on the floor under a nearby desk, but I decide to pick my battles, so I leave him there.

"I want *Interrupting Chicken*," Nick says, throwing down the book I've handed him.

"Nick, it doesn't matter which one you get right now," I say.

"Here." Kimberly hands him *Interrupting Chicken* and he hugs it to his chest.

"Miss Emery," Natalie says, "my uncle Robby, he ran his truck into a tree and he's in the hospital and my daddy said it's 'cause he dranked too many beers, and my momma got mad and told my daddy—"

"TMI, sweetheart." I cut her off, putting a finger over my lips. Mrs. Campbell always says it in such a kind voice that it doesn't hurt their feelings when she interrupts their long stories.

"Look at you," Jake says in a low voice beside me. "I didn't know you spoke Teacher."

I take a few steps away so the kids can't hear me. "I just don't have time to tune in to the Natalie Channel right now."

"I hear you." He grins, then looks again at my face. "Hey, Em, you okay?"

"I'm good," I tell him, and I'm surprised that it's the

truth, that I've somehow managed to channel Mrs. Campbell instead of my mom—at least for now. One of my greatest fears is that I'll react to every problem in life with anger and bitterness like my mom. I don't want to let my insecurity drive everyone away. I don't want to be unhappy and alone.

"Sorry I had to leave you," Jake says.

"It's okay. You had to help Mrs. Campbell." We haven't had a chance to talk since he got back to the room. "Jake, the security guard . . . Was he . . . ?"

"Didn't see him, and I didn't have time to ask." He shakes his head. "I just don't know."

"That's mine! I had it first." An argument erupts, this time between DeQuan and Tyler, and Jake moves to separate them.

I turn back to the kids. "Let's all see if we can count how many animals are in our books," I tell them, searching my brain for something to occupy them.

Olivia starts counting loudly.

I lean my face down close to hers and whisper, "Count to yourself, lovey."

She shifts into exaggerated silent mode, pointing to each animal and mouthing her count soundlessly. Honestly, they're heartbreakingly cute.

My love for these kids suddenly overwhelms me and my eyes fill with tears. I feel like I've come to know them so well in just a few short months. I can't let anything happen to them. We have to get them out of here. I turn away from them and move quickly, before I can lose my nerve, to speak to Stutts in the front of the room.

"Mr. Stutts, why don't you let the kids go?" Stutts looks up, surprised that I've addressed him. I'm surprised, too. "I know they're driving you crazy, and I can't promise how long I can keep them quiet. You can keep me and Jake."

"Just keep me," Jake chimes in, coming up behind me. "Look, my dad's the mayor. He has a lot of clout, and he's not going to let anything happen to me. You can use me to get what you want. Just let the kids and Emery go."

"Jake—" I try to interrupt.

"*Don't* tell me what to do," Stutts yells at us. "I don't need your help."

"You can think better if you don't have all this distraction," I try again.

As if on cue, Mason Mayfield III yells, "You're a poophead!" at Lewis, and Natalie starts to cry again over some slight, real or imagined. I turn back to shush them.

"If you let them go, I'll do everything I can to make sure you're heard," Jake says.

Stutts looks over at the kids. He paces, still keeping the door in his line of vision, the gun waving dangerously in his hand every time he speaks.

"No," he says. "Everybody shut up!"

I turn back to the kids. "Y'all keep counting." What would Mrs. Campbell do? "Whoever has the most animals in your book gets to be the line leader tomorrow." My bribe turns out to be the exact right thing to say. It seems to calm the overcharged atmosphere in the room—the idea that tomorrow will be a normal day and that we'll be choosing line leaders to go to lunch again.

"Do we count people?" Alicia asks. Good question. I look at Stutts, prowling like a mean wildcat.

"Sure, let's count humans as animals, too."

"What about bugs? Are they animals?" Tyler asks.

Geez, I never knew making up a game could have so many darn rules. "Sure, bugs count."

I'm touched by Jake's offer of himself as a hostage. I've never even heard him refer to himself before as the mayor's son. He hates it when anybody brings it up. I'm pretty sure it's the reason for a lot of the stuff he does—that and losing his mom.

I saw Mrs. Willoughby at the grocery store soon after I heard she had breast cancer. She had a bright blue scarf around her head with big hoop earrings, like she was trying to look all cheery, but her face was pale and there were dark circles under her eyes. I didn't know Jake well enough to talk to him then—it was before we started going out—but I heard from someone else just a few weeks later that things were bad. Even after we'd been together awhile, he didn't want to talk about her death—or her life, either. It was hard to get him to go there, but I knew he needed to.

I don't really know much about the marijuana bust.

Molly heard he and Cole and Hunter got pulled over and the cop searched the car. I don't think there was a lot of weed—but enough to get them arrested. I've never known Jake to smoke, but maybe it's his way of getting back at his dad—for getting remarried so fast. And to Christine, who makes everything worse than it needs to be.

CHAPTER 10

JAKE

I KNOW THERE ARE A LOT OF RUMORS about the drug thing this summer, but basically, what happened was, Cole and I went to pick up Hunter to get a milk shake after he had his wisdom teeth out. We had to wait for him to finish taking a shower. Cole says Hunter takes four showers a day—whenever he gets lonely, if you get the joke. Cole's a real comedian.

We always go to a place down the road called Dee's Burgers. Cole calls it Disease Burgers. So when we get there, Dee's isn't real crowded even though it's a Friday night. But Hunter doesn't want anybody to see him with his face all lopsided, so I park a little ways away from the door and bring the food out. We're just finished eating our burgers in the car—Hunter's drinking a shake—when Cole hauls out this baggie and some papers from his pocket and starts rolling a joint.

"Aw, naw, Cole, don't pull that shit out here," I tell him.

"It's for our boy Hunter, dude," Cole says. "Look at him; the man's in pain. Why are you such a pussy about weed, Willoughby?"

"I just don't wanna get busted, man. It's stupid to pull it out here."

"No, you're being an old lady. C'mon, Church Lady, lighten up."

"I believe you mean 'light up,'" Hunter says, holding his jaw.

"Look, I'm not gonna be one of those burnouts at school," I say. "Hell, half my first period business ed class last year was stoned outta their minds before they got to school every day."

"Hey, wait a minute," Cole says. "First semester? I was in that class."

"I rest my case. Look, wake 'n' bake is a bad way to live, if you ask me."

Cole lights up, inhales, then exhales with a big smile. He tries to pass it to me, but I shake my head, so he hands it back to Hunter.

"Just be careful, man," I tell them as Hunter looks over his shoulder, takes a hit, then passes it back to Cole. "All we need is for some cop to show up."

"Like that one?" Hunter asks. We all look back at the cruiser pulling into the parking lot.

"Shit, shit, shit," Cole mutters as we try to act normal while he frantically stabs out the j against his shoe. Hunter's fanning the air. "Don't look back at him. He'll know we're up to something." Cole pulls down the visor mirror and we watch a big bald-headed older cop get out of the car.

"He's lookin' over here. Go, go, go," Hunter says. "Get the fuck outta here."

I crank the car and throw it in reverse.

"Too late," I groan, watching in horror as the cop walks in our direction.

Cole opens the glove compartment and shoves the baggie inside.

"What the hell you doin'?" I whisper-yell. "You can't put that there!"

The cop is almost to the door.

"What do you want me to do with it?" he says, panicked.

"Shit, you know he's gonna smell it," I say. "Roll down the window on your side!"

"Too late," Hunter says, and I look up to find the policeman motioning for me to roll down mine.

"You boys havin' trouble?" he asks as I hit the window button, giving him my most innocent expression.

"No, sir, we were just headin' out," I say. *Please, God, just let us head out.*

"Mind if I see your license, young man?"

"Sure thing, Officer." Shit. The kiss-up's a dead giveaway. I don't even ask the obvious question about whether we're doing something wrong—since I already know the answer. The policeman takes my license, studies it, frowns, and leans down to look in at me. "You Mayor Willoughby's son?"

"Yes, sir."

And then I see the inevitable sniff test and I know it's all over.

I can see the guy struggling for a second. The decision of whether he wants to bust the mayor's son takes some thought. I hold my breath, hoping he'll decide it might be bad for his career.

"Smells like you boys been smokin' some dope in here." Apparently not a career cop.

"No, sir, we just had some burgers," Cole says.

"Ain't a burger in the world smells like that, son." Boy, this guy is slick.

"Uh, my friend just had his wisdom teeth out," Cole says, leaning over to speak to the cop. "They gave him some stuff to gargle with. Maybe that's what you're smelling." His bullshit is so lame, even *I'm* embarrassed.

"How 'bout you boys step out of the car?" Officer Slick requests with a smile.

We have no choice but to climb out and face our fate.

"Keep your hands where I can see 'em. That's it. Just put your hands on the vehicle," he says as Cole leans forward on the back of the car. People in the parking lot stare as we "assume the position."

"I'm gonna need you to spread 'em." He taps his flashlight on the inside of Cole's legs. "Just like that." He searches Cole's pockets and frisks him, patting down his upper body, then his pants legs and socks. He dumps Cole's wallet on top of the car and turns his attention to me. Soon the contents of my and Hunter's pockets are spread near Cole's.

"Sir, we were just getting a burger," Cole tries again. "None of us have ever been in any trouble."

"Then you got nothin' to worry about, sport." The policeman moves to the car and shines his flashlight around the seat and floor.

That damn glove compartment might as well be glowing with phosphorescent light. It's obviously the only hiding place there is. We're all sweatin' bullets by the time he reaches for the latch.

"Mind if I take a look in here?" he asks. It's a rhetorical question. Hunter's dad is a lawyer, and he's told us cops can search your car. All they have to do is say they smelled something, and they can look anywhere they want.

As soon as he punches the button, the plastic bag pops out like a damn jack-in-the-box. He opens it, sniffs the contents, and looks over at us.

"I believe you boys'll be takin' a little ride with me." No one says a word as we walk toward the squad car. Hunter's looking a little green and my legs feel like jelly.

Just as the cop opens the back door for us to get in, Hunter leans over and barfs on the ground. We all stand there and watch him puke. Finally, he says, "Sorry, I don't feel so good. It's probably the pain pills I'm taking."

"Got a little excited there, huh, pardner?" the cop says. "Just make sure you don't get vomit in my car."

Hunter nods to show he'll be all right, then gets a funny look on his face and pukes again.

"Aw, man," the cop says.

I'm tempted to track it on my shoes on purpose, but we step over the mess and get in the car.

The rest of that night is a blur of mug shots, jail cells, and the worst—calls to the 'rents. My dad barely speaks to me when he gets there, then all the way home in the car he yells at me about how stupid I am. We both know he's thinking about how this will affect his political career.

Before The Christine came along, things were good between me and Dad. We did stuff together every Saturday morning. It was our day—from the time I was, like, five or six. First we'd eat breakfast at Miss Ruby's; it's a down-home kinda place where local politicians and town bigwigs meet at what everyone calls the Liar's Table. We always ordered biscuits and gravy; I guess that's where my biscuit addiction started. My dad sat me at the table next to him, and when they were talking about some sports team or town squabble, he'd look at me and say, "What's your take on that, Jake?" After breakfast, we'd run errands—to the hardware store or, in the summer, to the farmer's market. When I got older, we threw a Frisbee in the park or went fishing or sometimes just hiking on one of the trails on Merritt Mountain a few miles away.

After Mom died, he tried to keep our tradition up, even though we'd been kicked in the gut. We still went somewhere every Saturday, just for an hour or so. But then The

Christine came along, and she decided she liked to have her coffee on the back deck with my dad on Saturdays and read the paper, which takes her pretty much all morning— because she's a brainless moron.

Fine by me. Dad and I don't have much to say to each other lately, anyway. I didn't really expect him to stand by me when I got in trouble. He just believed the worst—like everybody else.

So I got grounded that night for about a million years, and the worst thing about it was how happy it made The Christine. She'd been telling my dad for months what a loser I am. I hate like hell I proved her right.

CHAPTER 11
Emery

"Look, Miss Emery, mine has eleventy-three animals," Kimberly announces proudly, holding up a picture book. Great, how am I going to reward the winner of the animal counting contest in a room full of made-up numbers?

"Terrific, Kimberly," I tell her. "Anyone else have more?" No one speaks up. "Then Kimberly is the winner—with eleventy-three animals in her book." I'm not waiting for anyone to argue.

"Eleventy-three's not a number," Alicia complains, very irritated.

"It is today, Alicia. By God, eleventy-three is a number today."

I'm exhausted, and I haven't even had a chance to show Jake what I found in Mrs. Campbell's purse. When I was searching for insulin and found her phone, I thought maybe it was dead, but when I touched it, it lit up. She was totally convincing when she told Stutts her cell phone was broken. Talk about a poker face—Willa Campbell is a world-class bluffer.

It would be hard to text or e-mail for help without Stutts seeing, but it might be possible to use it to bring up Internet on the computer. I remember Jake's brother doing some kind of tethering thing once, so maybe Jake'll know how. If we could figure out a way to get Stutts to let us use the computer, we might be able to communicate with the police.

Mason whines, "I'm hungry. I wanna go outside. Do we get to go home today?" Being locked in a room with Stutts all morning is starting to wear on all of us. The kids need a diversion. I get up and walk to where Stutts is sitting.

"Look, we're trying to keep the kids quiet, but it would help if they had something fun to do. Will you let us see if there are any games on the teacher's computer? They could take turns."

"No computer," he growls.

"We can unhook the Internet. It's just that blue cord that connects to the wall right there. The school system's too cheap to pay for wireless."

Jake's looking kinda puzzled, not sure why the computer game idea is important, but he goes with it. He walks over and pulls the cord from the wall and puts it on the table near Stutts. "No connection." Jake points to the computer. "See for yourself."

Stutts doesn't answer. Simon and Kenji are looking at

him pleadingly. Patrick sinks lower in his seat; he's sure he won't be included in any group activities. I notice he rarely looks at his father.

Stutts glances over as Jake opens the programs and finds several games. "Just games, man," he says to Stutts. "They'll keep the kids out of your hair."

Stutts grunts and turns away, which seems to be, amazingly, a yes, or at least an "I don't care." The kids are all waving their hands. Mason's yelling, "Me, me! Pick me. I wanna go first."

"Hold on a second." I reach for Mrs. C.'s flowerpots.

Every morning when the kids come in, they pick up the popsicle stick "flower" with their name on it from the box on the table and stick it in the hot lunch pot or the cold lunch pot. That way Mrs. C. can send in the lunch count to the office without having to ask. She also keeps the flowers on her desk to use when she needs to choose someone for a job or to answer a question. She picks a flower and reads the name, then puts it back in the box for the next day. She told us that, by the end of each day, everyone's been chosen for something.

I draw three names: Nick, Tyler, and Kaela. They bounce to the front of the room, and several other kids pout.

"Don't worry. Everybody'll get a turn. And the rest of us can work on the coloring puzzles some more."

"You said you were gonna read us a book," Natalie says.

"As soon as we finish the puzzles." I don't trust my shaky voice to read aloud just yet.

Stutts moves a chair—an adult-size one—halfway between us and the door, still watching the hall. He looks so nervous. I watch his hand on the gun and hope he has better control than he seems to.

"Mason's messing with Mr. Worley," Alicia calls out from the back of the room.

"Mason, go back to your seat," I say, sighing.

"I hate you," he says to Alicia as he passes her desk. "I hope you move to Pluto."

"Pluto's not even a planet anymore." She sticks out her tongue.

"Hey, you two, that's enough," I tell them. They can't help it that they don't really understand what could happen here. I have trouble comprehending it myself.

The natives are restless, so I offer a bribe. "The first three finished can choose something from the prize basket."

And they're back to work. Toys and treats always do the job.

Stutts is leaning back in his chair in front of the fall leaves display on the wall—deep red and orange and yellow ones the kids brought in for Mrs. C. to help them iron between pieces of waxed paper. His eyes are half closed, and he's dividing his attention between the door and the computer. The shadows under his eyes look like bruises; I doubt he sleeps much. You could almost feel sorry for him—except that he's holding a gun on a room full of little kids.

Patrick's head is on the table, one arm bent to form a pillow. Stutts reaches over and opens his son's backpack.

He pulls out Patrick's jacket, wads it up, and pushes it under his head. Patrick burrows into the soft fleece. The un-expected tenderness surprises me—and motivates me to try to make a connection with him.

Screw your courage to the sticking place, Emery. It's now or never. I walk to the front, pull a chair within a few feet of Stutts, and sit down, my knees shaking a little. He looks over at me, then back at the door. But he doesn't tell me to go away. I can feel Jake's eyes on me from across the room.

"Patrick's a great kid," I say to him.

He glances at his son. His face softens just a little. "Yep."

"He doesn't talk a lot, but he always knows the right an-swer if you call on him."

No comment. I feel a little silly talking to myself, but I keep going.

"You must read to him a lot." I look around the room, like I don't care if he answers or not—no pressure.

"My wife—she does."

Long silence. Nick lets out a whoop of victory and the other kids at the computer moan. "Your turn, Kaela," Jake says.

"My parents always read to me when I was little," I say.

Stutts squints his eyes like he's trying to focus on some-thing across the room.

"You read much?" I ask him.

He shrugs, then says without looking at me, "Tom Clancy, stuff like that."

"Did you always want to join the military?"

"No." He sighs and shifts in his chair like he wishes I'd go away. But he doesn't run me off. "Didn't know what else to do," he mumbles, "when I graduated."

Long pause.

"I guess you've seen a lot . . . over there. A lot of bad stuff."

"What're you trying to say?" He turns to look at me, his eyes cold, his voice hard. "You think I'm crazy?"

"No, no, not at all." I keep my voice casual, trying not to show how much he scares me. "I just think that would have a big effect on anybody, that's all."

"You could say that." He's watching the door again.

I wait.

"You know what an IED is, kid?" he finally says, glancing over at me.

"An explosive device."

"You got it. Improvised explosive device. Shit'll blow. You. Up. It's packed into empty soda cans, paper cups, plastic bags, food containers, dead animal carcasses—you name it. People think you can just avoid stuff in the road when you're driving over there. You know why you can't?"

I shake my head, trying not to show my surprise that he's talking to me.

"Because there's trash everywhere. The roads are lined with garbage. No way to know which garbage'll kill you. You ride down the road looking as hard as you can for the stuff that's gonna make you dead—and you know all the time you can't tell it's comin' until it's too late." He glances at me with a sneer. "So if I seem a little jumpy to you, princess, you'll have to excuse me."

"I didn't say you were." I'm navigating my own land mines here. "I just don't know what it's like there. I'm just asking you . . . because I'm interested."

"What do you want to know?"

"About the people. Were you able to get along with the Iraqis?"

"Yes, I've spent time with Iraqi families in their own living rooms, talking about their culture. I've given their children candy and treated their women with respect. I've had little old men shake my hand and thank me for helping them. I'm not some meathead who goes around busting in doors and intimidating people, if that's what you think."

"No, I never—"

"That said," he cuts me off and continues, "if you try to kill me or my buddies, that makes you the enemy, and you are going down. I don't care who you are or what your religion is or isn't; we'll hunt you down and we will take you out. That is nonnegotiable."

His tone is steely; the volume escalates. Jake looks up, but I shake my head slightly. A tense silence hangs in the air.

I try another angle. "Were you able to talk to your family much?"

"Had Internet most of the time, and I phoned some." His eyes are heavy—from fatigue or booze, I'm not sure which.

I try not to look at the gun—or think about his sweaty hands.

"How long were you there?"

"This last time, a year—but I was there two years starting in 2005."

"Where's 'there'? What part?"

"Baghdad." He runs a hand across his cropped hair.

"I guess there were a lot of things you can't ever really describe."

He stares at me, narrowing his eyes. "Look, I don't want to talk about it, okay?"

"Sure, no problem, I understand." I stand up and walk over casually to read the kids' papers hanging on the wall. Mrs. Campbell helped them write out their Rules for Life. She likes for them to be free to write without worrying too much about spelling. The one closest to the window is Tyler's. His rules are:

1. Dont leev yur bike in the dry way.
2. Dont poop in the bat tub.
3. Dont fergit to pee befor hid and seek.

The obsession with potty business makes me smile, but the narrow scope of their problems before now tugs at my heart.

The rules changed today.

I can hear car doors slamming outside, and I wonder if there are news cameras. Hensonville's a sleepy little town.

A purse snatching at the mall gets top billing on our one local TV station's nightly news, and police don't have much to do besides stop speeders . . . until today.

When kids start school here, moms worry about whether they'll have somebody to sit with at the lunch table, or whether they'll have a nice teacher—not whether they'll come home.

My mother must be climbing the walls by now. I glance at Jake at the computer and wish I had a way to let her know I'm all right.

I turn back to Stutts and say casually, "I'm just going to fix these blinds where they're twisted."

He looks at the small gap in the blinds and says, "Go ahead."

I reach for the problem spot, which is, conveniently, at eye level.

What I see takes my breath away.

There are police cars everywhere, people running, news trucks lining the curb, and SWAT team guys suiting up beside a dark-colored van. I'm sure we don't have a SWAT team; they must have brought them in from somewhere else. Yellow crime scene tape has been used to block off the front of the building, and the parking lot's been cleared.

There are two single-file lines of kids walking fast out of the building, with teachers and policemen walking beside them. They're evacuating the school—getting as many kids as they can out of the reach of Brian Stutts. I'm guessing they decided not to empty the classrooms in our wing.

And then I see something that nearly drops me to my knees.

Four ambulances.

All lined up in a row in front of the school.

Waiting for victims of the shooter. Waiting to take them—us—to the hospital. Or to . . . My head spins, the scene blurs, and I reach out to steady myself on the windowsill. I take deep breaths, fighting the spell that threatens to pull me under.

I turn to look at the children behind me working quietly, mostly unaware that their lives could be cut short at the whim of a madman. *Dear God, please help us find a way out of this.*

I realize if I'm going to help these kids, I need to concentrate on the here and now. I straighten out the blinds and walk away from the window, but I'm careful not to look at Stutts. Maybe I was a fool to try to strike up a conversation with him when SWAT team guys are suiting up to protect themselves from him. My head tells me to stay away, but my gut says I have to make him see us as people, so he'll know who we are. Maybe then it'll be harder for him to—

I can't think about that. I won't let that picture into my head.

CHAPTER 12

JAKE

I'M TRYING LIKE HELL TO BE INTER-
ested in the kids' computer games, 'cause I hate
when grown-ups give you those little "uh-huh,"
"that's nice" comments when they're not really
paying attention. But my mind is racing—if I could
talk to Cole, he'd figure out what we should do.
People don't give Cole a lot of credit for smarts,
but most of the time he's great at getting out of
trouble—he's had *lots* of experience. He definitely
comes through in an emergency. Emery says I
spend too much time with Cole, and my dad
thinks so, too. After we got into trouble this summer, my dad had some line about if you hang out
in a barber shop, you're eventually gonna get a
haircut.

Emery just doesn't understand our friendship,
but Cole's my boy. He checks in with me every few
days to see if I need anything, he'd beat the crap
out of anybody who said a word against me, and if

there's a crisis, he usually has me laughing like a hyena by the end of the disaster. He's been great since the weed thing; I think he's trying to make it up to me for not taking the blame, even though he never apologized.

Emery gives me a look from the back of the room that makes me wonder if there's something going on outside. What the hell was she trying to do anyway, talking to Stutts? Does she think they're going to be buddies or something? This ain't the freakin' *Oprah* show. The best course of action is to stay as far away from that guy as possible.

Her eyes have that intense look they get. They study you like they'll swallow you whole. A shaman's eyes, I told her once. I don't know if she can see the future, but she can damn sure see anything you're trying to hide.

We started going out after we met up at a party at Tab's house. We'd been talking in art class, and okay, I'm not gonna lie, I liked her a lot. This'll sound really cheesy, but for the first time since my mom died, I actually woke up feeling pretty good just knowing I'd see Emery when I got to school.

I'll admit I felt a little off base with her at first. Emery has a low tolerance for bullshit, so I knew my usual tricks weren't gonna work. But I liked it that I was never sure what she was gonna say—and that I could count on her to always tell me the truth.

Things were going good. But then something happened. Okay, full disclosure: I was a jerk, I admit it, but when Stacey Jordan called and invited me to Heather Raby's lake house for a party that Sunday afternoon, I told myself she was just being friendly. I mean, senior girls don't go after junior guys. It wasn't a date. We didn't even ride out there together. She just asked if I wanted to meet her there. Seriously, Stacey Jordan—who's gonna turn *that* down?

Emery was working on a research paper that weekend, so I didn't mention the party. Stacey and I hung out all afternoon, mostly with everybody else. I had a few beers, and then a few more, and Stacey was being pretty friendly, especially when she asked if I wanted to take a walk in the woods with her. Sure, I felt a little guilty about making out with her, but like Cole said, Emery didn't own me. It wasn't like I'd made some big commitment to her.

I had a lot to drink—way more than I should have—and I think I said something to Stacey like I wanted to get to know her better, and I guess she took it the wrong way, 'cause the next thing I know, Stacey's posted on Facebook that we're in a relationship. Hell, I don't know why she did it. Who knows why girls do shit like that?

I knew something was up when Tab called me at one in the morning and said, "Asshole," and hung up.

I was waiting at Emery's locker when she got to school that day. I tried to talk to her. I told her Stacey didn't mean anything to me, but that just made her madder. She wouldn't even look at me. She just opened her locker, pulled down the picture I'd taken of us on that first day of art class, tore it in little pieces, dropped it at my feet, and walked away. She wouldn't answer my phone calls—I tried for days.

I did everything I could to make it up to Emery. I even

wrote her a long note about how I felt about her. I've never been able to talk to any other girl the way I could talk with Emery. We always had a great time together. And even though we never said we were exclusive or anything, to be honest, what I did was pretty low. I mean, I'd definitely be pissed off if she'd done it to me.

I can blame it on the beer, but it's a pretty sorry excuse if you get right down to it. The thing is, if you have to think about whether something's right or wrong, it's probably wrong.

Bottom line, I screwed up. I wanted another chance to make things right, so I left the note on her car while she was at an Honor Society meeting at school.

And then I waited. I was pretty sure that note would do the trick. I mean, hell, *I'd* go out with me if I read the stuff in there. It was an *epic* apology.

And then I waited some more. Two days passed, then three. I started to call her again after a week with no word, but what was the point? I'd said everything I had to say. When she never even bothered to answer me, I knew we were finished.

I was a complete jerk, but everybody makes mistakes. I just wish there was a way for Emery and me to start over.

That's why I was happy about getting partnered with her for tutoring, even though I knew she wouldn't make it easy. I was hoping I could spend time with her again and maybe show her I'm not a total dick.

"Heard you got put with Emery Austin for tutoring," Cole said after school the day the list was posted. News travels fast.

"Too bad she hates my guts," I said.

"She doesn't really," Bethany, his latest girlfriend, said, patting me on the shoulder.

Bethany was kinda rubbing my shoulder, so I moved away from her. I'm a friendly guy, and girls get the wrong idea sometimes. Emery makes fun of me 'cause I got voted Biggest Flirt in the yearbook freshman year, but sometimes I get the feeling she doesn't think it's funny.

Who knows how girls think? Guys are like simple machines—we're pulleys and levers that react to whatever happens right then, and then we're over it. Girls are complex computer systems—complicated motherboards no one can understand. All I know is, it seems like every time I pay attention to somebody, the girl has me practically engaged by the next day. Look, I just like to have a good time. I'm not interested in getting too serious—with anybody. Well, with almost anybody.

CHAPTER 13

Emery

"I have to go to the bathroom," Rose says suddenly, tugging at my hand. It's the first time she's preferred me over Jake—this is a girl thing.

"Me too," Natalie says.

I turn to Stutts, but he frowns and shakes his head before I can even ask.

This is going to be an ongoing problem with eighteen first graders. What are we going to do?

I look around the room for tools to build a makeshift bathroom.

"You know what this place needs?" I turn to Rose. "A private potty. Jake, can you get me one of those big plastic tubs up there—with a lid?" I reach up and lift the huge corkboard off the wall. Jake comes over to help me, but it's not very heavy, just awkward.

"What's that for?" Rose asks.

"A wall. A wall for our very own bathroom," I tell her. Rose looks doubtful.

"I'll hold this up in front of you while you use the plastic tub as a toilet," I say. She looks horrified. "Hey, it'll be fun— just like camping. Haven't you ever used the bathroom in the woods?"

She shakes her head.

"Well, you have missed a real treat, I'm telling you." I'm acting like peeing in a plastic tub in a room full of people is an amazing adventure. "Alicia, hand me that Kleenex box, will you?"

"My cousin showed me how to go without getting my clothes wet," Natalie announces. "I'll go first."

"Awesome," I say. For once I'm grateful for Natalie's need for the spotlight. "And will you show Rose?"

Rose frowns. "Don't worry," I tell her, "no one can see you with this big wall up. It's a little easier for the boys to go to the bathroom in the classroom, but we girls'll manage just fine." I push a chair behind the bulletin board wall. "Here's something to hold on to if you need it for balance."

Natalie's skills as a toilet tutor are in high demand. Three other girls line up immediately, and then four of the boys. Jake holds the wall for the guys.

"Nice work, Teach," Jake says as I put the lid on the "potty."

"I just hope you don't have to hold the wall for me," I tell him.

"You need to go?" he asks. "I got you covered."

"Not just yet. But thanks."

He helps me get them all settled back on their carpet, and I sit on the floor with them, watching them color. The tension shows in their small bodies. DeQuan grips the crayons so hard he breaks one, Kenji's tiny tennis shoes tap the air anxiously, Alicia fiddles nervously with the button on her shirt, and Mason Mayfield III is drumming on a notebook with a pencil. At every sound in the quiet room, heads bob and eyes dart.

Olivia is chewing on her fingers. I reach over and pull her hand away and point to her painted nails. "Pretty," I whisper, and she smiles and drops her hands into her lap. Carlos cracks his knuckles, then gives me an *oops* look, like he's been told at home not to do that.

I try to remember what I was like at age six—back in the days when I thought the moon was made of cheese and buffalo wings came from buffaloes and you could dig your way to China in the sandbox. That was about the age Molly and I rubbed dandelions all over our heads, not knowing the bees would chase us. Did I understand real danger?

I always felt so safe when my dad read to me in our big upholstered rocking chair, the one with soft, sink-down pillows and big cushy arms. It was covered in plush red velvet—the kind you could dig your toes into. Mom complained that we'd rubbed half the fabric off the arms, but I loved snuggling with my dad in it. It was our special place.

He read all my favorite books to me, and I'd fall asleep on his broad chest, the vibration of his deep voice rumbling against my cheek. Sometimes he sang to me, or just hummed as I drifted off.

And then one day in third grade, I came home from school—he had already moved out by then—and my mother had recovered our chair in a stiff plaid material. I just stood there staring at what was left of it and feeling my heart break into a thousand tiny pieces.

DeQuan glances up to see if I'm noticing his good behavior and I give him a thumbs-up. Jake laughs at the way the kids are always showing me stuff. And telling me stories about their dog dying or their grandpa being in the hospital or their mom getting mad or their dad getting fired. With all the trauma at home, it's easy to understand why they can't wait to get to school. It's one way life with my mother and her nightly running monologue has paid off: I'm a very good listener.

It seems like kids are always waiting for something— waiting for a bike without training wheels or for a trip to the beach. Waiting for the puppy they've been promised. They shouldn't be waiting to see if they get to go home from school. Or waiting to be released as hostages.

I try not to think about what would have happened if Jake and I hadn't been here when Mrs. Campbell passed out. I reach over and squeeze Kenji's hand. His smile is a little wobbly. Rose is watching Jake. He has a way of putting people at ease, even in the worst situation possible. That trait was a blessing and a curse when we were together. He always talked to everyone, and sometimes I felt a little left out.

When Jake and I had art class together second semester, there was a lot of downtime to chat. Tab and Molly can talk to anybody, but before Jake, I swear I couldn't form a complete sentence if a hot guy was around.

Jake made it easy. For that whole first month of art class, we talked every day for pretty much the whole period. It was hard to believe the relationship I'd fantasized about since that ninth grade cafeteria rescue was becoming a reality. Tab's birthday party, the day after Valentine's Day, was the first time it was just the two of us.

The party was getting rowdy that night, and I slipped out onto the screened-in porch when the guys broke into Tab's dad's liquor cabinet. I was listening to the rain in the dark and suddenly he was there.

"Not much of a party girl?" he asked.

"There's a pretty nice party out here," I told him, just as a flash of lightning lit our faces.

"Am I invited?"

"If you want to be."

We talked for over an hour. Jake is so completely focused on you when you're talking to him, it's almost unnerving. I've never seen him text or check Facebook when he's involved in a conversation. He makes you feel like everything you're saying is important to him.

When I finally stood up to leave, he grabbed my hand. "Don't go, Emery," he said. The way he said my name lit up places inside me like pinball pegs.

"Curfew. My mom's a tyrant."

He walked me to my car in the rain, holding his jacket over our heads. It seemed so natural when he leaned down to kiss me. Then he held on to me for a long time, both of us getting soaked and not caring. I felt like he was telling me something without words; I understood that he needed me to be there just then.

"I'll call you," he said, and I told myself I'd be okay if he didn't.

My phone rang before I was out of Tab's driveway. I looked back to see him standing on the steps smiling at me, getting drenched.

"What's up?" he asked, like we hadn't just talked for an hour.

I talked to him all the way home, while I got ready for bed, and after I turned out the lights. We talked about everything and nothing—until the sun came up.

And every night after that.

For weeks.

My mom would flip out if she knew how little sleep I got. She obsesses about my not getting enough rest. I went to his baseball games all through spring and we went out to eat after. On weekends we went to movies or he came over. We sat together at lunch at school and he walked me to my car every day.

But it was those late-night conversations I loved most. I told him things I'd never told anybody—mostly about my parents' divorce, about how I used to hide under the bed with my stuffed animals when they were fighting.

And after a while, he opened up to me about his mom dying. About how he helped her buzz her head when her hair started falling out after chemo. He said they tried to make a joke of it, but he went in his room and cried after he was done, and later he heard her crying, too.

He told me how he read to her when she was sick. She said the sound of his voice made the pain go away. But, toward the end, when the cancer was worse, she'd fall asleep as soon as he started.

I've never talked that way to anyone before—not even to Tab and Molly.

Molly was all excited about me and Jake. She said it was "so Edward and Bella"; she's a big fan of the Twilight books. I wasn't sure how to take that—being compared to an ordinary, clumsy girl in love with a gorgeous, shimmering boy. I never felt ordinary when I was with Jake. He told me I was beautiful in a way that sent me back to my mirror with fresh eyes. I wanted to see what made him choose me. I knew others were looking at me differently, too. It was a new experience to see envy in other girls' eyes.

Tab never trusted Jake. She said he was superficial and full of himself. She didn't like the way he kidded around with people. She didn't think it was funny when he'd do things like put a book on erectile dysfunction in Hunter's backpack when we were all at the public library. Then, when the alarms went off, Hunter had to hand off the book to the librarian—in front of everybody. It seemed like a pretty harmless prank to me.

I thought Tab just didn't understand Jake. He has this charisma that draws people to him. He tunes in to everybody in the room in a way that's hard to explain. I've watched him seek out the awkward person at a party who's standing in a corner and strike up a big conversation, and he always acted like he was having a ball talking to my mother when she fed him snacks in our kitchen. He did magic tricks with the little boy next door I babysit for and brought bones to Molly's dog. He sincerely likes people and he just makes these instant connections, even with total strangers. He'll chat up anybody—at ball games, the mall, wherever.

Sometimes I wonder what it would be like to be that easy with people—to always know the right thing to say and to feel like you fit in wherever you are. I was so flattered by his attention, I let my guard down. I believed in him. I trusted him.

But in the end, I guess Tab was right about him.

She called that night to tell me she'd heard Jake was with Stacey Jordan at the lake party, and that Stacey had posted on Facebook that she and Jake were in a relationship. After we'd been going out constantly for almost four months—February, March, April, and part of May. Even though we'd never said we were exclusive or anything, he had to know how I felt about him.

It was a shitty thing to do.

He met me at my locker before school the next morning, and when he didn't even try to deny what happened, I knew it was true.

"So you *were* making out with Stacey Jordan?"

"Well, I wouldn't call it making out."

"What *would* you call it, Jake?"

"Emery, she doesn't mean anything to me."

"And that's supposed to make me feel better? That you cheated on me and you don't even care about her?"

"I didn't really see it as cheating. I mean, we never really—"

I walked away. I didn't want to hear the rest.

We never really were exclusive? Or did "we never really" mean something else?

Jake had pressured me about sex during the last few weeks we were together. Even though we did a lot of other stuff—things I'd never done with any other guy—I just wasn't ready for that last big step. I was crazy about him and he knew that, but I didn't feel like I'd known him long enough.

Or maybe there was a small part of me that didn't trust him to stay.

Jake acted like I had no right to be mad. Maybe he was trying to tell me it wasn't really a breakup if we were never together. Apparently, I made the whole thing up and he never thought of me as his girlfriend at all—which makes me the lamest person ever.

That didn't stop me from completely falling apart when it was over. I hid out in my bedroom listening to angsty emo music in the dark and sleeping for the better part of a week and a half, until Molly had enough and dragged me out.

"You know, Emery," she told me, "a lot of guys do something stupid when they're afraid they're getting too serious and it scares the crap out of them. Maybe that's what happened with Jake. Maybe he cares about you *too* much instead of not enough."

"I don't think so, Mols." It was typical of Molly to try to put a positive spin on things. "I have to face the truth; it's over."

The worst part was knowing all the places I couldn't avoid him during the school day. My peripheral vision went into overdrive, and I was painfully aware of his position in the lunchroom or hallway or even the school parking lot. And I kept waiting for him to show up with Stacey Jordan or Callie Edwards. But he didn't.

I skipped art for four days, until Mrs. Hicks stopped me in the hall to tell me she was going to have to write me up. So I sat in the back for the last two weeks of school and tried not to look at him.

After I had the summer to piece my life back together, I was really looking forward to senior year. I knew I'd see him, but I felt like I was ready to deal with it and get on with my life. And then I got stuck with him as a tutoring partner.

I look over at him laughing with the kids at the computer.

"Are we gonna get to go home when the bell rings?" Nick is asking him, his face serious above his SpongeBob SquarePants shirt.

"Same as always—when the bell rings," Jake says confidently.

"That bell rings, I'ma be outta sight," Carlos says, looking up from his coloring to join their conversation.

"That's right, Dy-no-mite," DeQuan chimes in with the rhyming game.

"That's right, Bud Light," Jake adds without thinking, distracted by the computer game. I look up, shocked, and Jake gives me an *uh-oh* face, which makes me laugh, and pretty soon we're all giggling at the complete inappropriateness of his rhyme. We're so stressed, we can't think straight. I'm pretty sure I catch sight of a grin on Patrick's face, but Stutts seems zoned out. He doesn't tune in to the conversation at all.

"Do you drink beer?" Tyler asks.

"No," Jake answers, "and you shouldn't, either. That stuff's not good for you."

"I tasted my dad's one time," Carlos says, "and it was nasty."

"Exactly. Nasty stuff that makes you do dumb things."

He glances up at me with a regretful half smile. "Dumb things you'll be sorry for later."

I look away.

Jake looks over at Kenji, who's daydreaming a little. "Right, Batman?"

"Right, Robin," Kenji says without missing a beat.

"I wanna do something else," Mason Mayfield III says. "These puzzles are no fun."

"*What?*" Jake says. "Those puzzles are *awesome*! Those puzzles are more fun than, um, than March Madness." He grins at me. "Ask Miss Emery how much I love March Madness."

Jake practically camped out in my den last spring, intent on convincing me that my life was incomplete without a working knowledge of college basketball. I picture him sprawled on our couch, and suddenly scenes of the two of us replay in my mind—strung together like the wall quilt of kids' drawings that hangs above Mrs. Campbell's desk, linked with black yarn through paper-punch holes. Pictures of hikes and picnics and dinners and movies and laughter and touches and kisses. Pieces of the past.

Damn it, play fair, Willoughby. Those days are over.

CHAPTER 14

JAKE

"OKAY, NEXT THREE AT THE COM-puter are"—I draw three more names from the flowerpot—"Mason, Anna-Caroline, and Janita." The kids switch places with the others, and Mason Mayfield III elbows his way in front of the girls. I probably should get on him about his manners, but I'm just too tired to care. I'm picking my battles right now.

Emery's giving me weird looks across the room. I wish I knew what she's thinking. One minute we're laughing with the kids, and the next second she's giving me the evil eye.

Let me tell you, that girl can get a shit-ton of mileage out of the silent treatment. After that day she found out about Stacey, she refused to speak to me again, ever. Once I admitted I'd kissed Stacey Jordan, she was *done* with discussion.

I guess I can't really blame her. I'm the biggest screwup ever. Emery knows it. My friends know it.

My dad knows it. He didn't exactly say it that way, the night I got arrested, but he did plenty of yelling, and it was tough to see how disappointed he was.

Of course, The Christine went nuts. She still brings it up constantly. It's been over three months now, and I still can't leave the house without her telling my dad I can't be trusted. It's like it's her mission in life to remind him I'm a hardened criminal.

Last week he asked me to drop him at work because his car was in the shop. His cell phone rang that stupid ringtone she put on of some lame oldies song that's "their song." He answered, then listened without saying a word for, I swear, about five minutes, and then he hung up.

"What did she say about me?" I asked.

"Nothing," he said. He reached over and turned up the radio. "She just wants me to be mad at you." Then he rolled down the window and started whistling, like he didn't want to talk about her or me. Sometimes I wonder what that woman does for him that makes it worth putting up with her. Wait—I don't want to know. I *really* don't want to know.

Emery said something once about my dad that made sense to me. We were on the golf course at night. I used to work there on weekends, so I stole the key to a cart to surprise her with a late-night picnic. I'm not very good at organizing, so the food was mostly chips and cookies and some peanut-butter crackers, but she loved it.

We were lying on a blanket looking for the constellations and I said, "What I don't get is, how can a guy who's been with someone like my mom choose to be with The Christine? There couldn't possibly be two more different people."

"Maybe that's the point," she said. "He knows he can't have that again—what he had with her. So he's making sure what he has now is so different, he won't feel bad when it doesn't even come close."

It was better than anything I'd been able to come up with.

"I didn't even know he was thinking about dating until I saw that Internet match thing on his computer," I told her. "It seems like he could have waited at least a year."

"Some people just aren't meant to be alone," she said.

I remember the crickets were chirping that night, and we could hear a bullfrog croaking down by the pond. It was so damn peaceful out there.

"The worst part about losing Mom," I told her, "was she left us before she left us."

"What do you mean?" she asked.

"Those last two months, she stayed in her bedroom and hardly ever came out. I mean, I know she was sick and needed to rest—I'm not completely selfish. But it was more than that. It was like she didn't want to talk to us."

"The same thing happened with my grandmother," she said. "The hospice nurse told us people withdraw when they're dying. It's too painful to think about leaving the people they love, so they pull away to keep from hurting so bad.

It's a journey you have to make on your own, and closing yourself off from everybody is how you get yourself ready to do it."

"I just figured she didn't want me around."

Emery was quiet for a minute, then she said, "I think your mom loved you like crazy for as long as she could—until she had to let you go."

I guess I have to find a way for that to be enough.

I nudge Mason over to give the girls a turn, and he pouts. Emery raises her eyebrows across the room. It's like she knows when I'm thinking about my mom. The truth is, it happens all the time no matter what's going on—even when there's a man with a gun in the room.

"Miss Emery, come look at my score," Janita says.

Emery walks to the computer. "Awesome, Janita," she says. "Hey, when you finish this game, you guys come color with the rest of the class." They groan, and she adds, "There might be enough prizes for everybody."

She turns to me. "You wanna take a break before I send the next three kids to play?" she asks.

I know her well enough to know something's up, so I rush Janita and Anna-Caroline a little and send them back to where the others are.

When she sits next to me, I ask her in a low voice, "What the hell were you doing talking to him a little while ago?"

"Just trying to make a connection, calm down," she says, glancing over to make sure the kids' chatter will cover us.

"*Not* a good idea. That man is dangerous."

"Oh, really? Thanks for the tip, Jake. I had no idea."

She slides something toward me—a smartphone.

Emery leans in to point at something on the computer screen, but she's switching on the phone with her other hand. I glance down at the "Silent" icon; she's already turned the sound off.

"It's too risky to text," she whispers. "Any way we might use it to get Internet on the computer?"

"I haven't had a chance, with the kids up here, to see if there's any wireless capability. If this phone's set up to act as a mobile Wi-Fi hot spot, we can use it like a modem." I pull a notepad over the phone to hide it.

"I'm gonna go help the kids color," she says loud enough for Stutts to hear.

"Sounds good," I say, stretching like I'm bored.

Stutts watches her sit with the kids, and then shifts his eyes back to the door. He doesn't seem to be paying attention to me.

I search for a mobile hotspot icon. Yes. There it is. I switch it on, activate the Wi-Fi, and check the computer monitor for networks. Crap, please don't ask me for a password. I don't have a clue what— Great, the phone tells me how to access the network that pops up by entering the phone number as the password. It even tells me the phone number—nice.

Here we go. I hold my breath.

There it is. Beautiful! I'm online.

Without looking over at Stutts, I adjust the screen toward me very casually so there's no way he can see it. The keyboard's hidden behind a pile of books. I pull up Facebook. Chat's quicker than e-mail.

What time is it? 10:25. Good timing. Cole's in computer apps this period and he's usually online. I glance at Stutts; he's still watching the door.

Facebook log in. Done. I hit the chat bar. Be there, Cole . . .

Success! Cole Garrison is available to chat.

I type: *Cole, you there? I need help.*

Cole's profile pic pops up with: *hey bro where u?*

lincoln elementary. listen a crazy man with a gun is holding us hostage.

good one dude

no srsly. can you turn on the news?

no shit man? yr not dickin with me?

for real, i need yr help.

name it jake

*can you get mr.chapman? need him to help me talk
to the cops here to see what i need to do.*

hang on bro

There's a long pause while I wait for Cole to get our
principal. C'mon, Cole, don't leave me hangin'.

And then he's back: *mrs d went to turn on tv next door,
said shes sending me to the office if im making it up*

hurry. not sure how long i can talk.

Stutts eyes me from across the room so I do a little fist
pump like I've just scored. He turns to watch Emery with
the kids.

ok shes back. called office, chap is on the way.

thx cole. i owe u

u ok man?

yes but he shot a security guard.

shit—dude shootin people? who is he?

a soldier home from iraq. really messed up.

This is Mr. Chapman. I've got Chief Walker on phone. Is everyone ok there?

we're ok for now. the guy stutts doesnt know i have internet. i may have to shut down fast.

Are the children ok?

yes emerys got kids sitting on floor in back.

Jake, no one is hurt?

the security guard who got shot. can you tell us if hes ok?

Chief says he's in surgery. Is the shooter alone? Chief wants to know what he wants.

yes. alone. says he just wants to take his son. hes in this class. patrick.

How many children are still in the room?

18

Can you describe the gun for me? Does he have any other weapons?

a pistol, dont know type. i guess he could
have another gun—or a knife, but i havent
seen one.

Where is Stutts now?

in chair near door. watching the door.

Is there any other information you can give me?

he said his wife wont let him see his kid. if you
could find her and get her on the phone she
might help.

Chief says the police are already talking with her.

is there something we should do here?

Don't be a hero, Jake. Nothing risky. Just try to keep
him calm.

gotta go.

Chief says you should assume he will shoot. Don't
underestimate this guy.

k

They want to know if there's any way you can get him to release the kids?

tried. will try again.

I can feel Stutts watching me, so I close the screen and bring the games back up. Then I stand up and yawn and stretch and walk to the back.

"Good job, Kimberly," I say, looking over her shoulder.

"Is mine good?" Abbey asks.

"It's terrific." I smile. "That is some mighty fine coloring, ladies."

I glance over at Patrick. He's very still, watching the others color together. I walk to Mrs. Campbell's printer, pull a blank sheet of paper from the tray, and hold it up for him to see. He looks puzzled until I lay it on her desk and quickly turn it into a paper airplane. I aim it toward him and his face lights up. When I launch it, we both wait to see where it will land. I must be livin' right, because damn if that airplane doesn't sail in a beautiful arc, just like I'd planned it that way, landing right on the table in front of Patrick. He picks it up and grins at me, then looks over at his dad.

Stutts watches us, then turns away a little to take a quick pull from the flask in his pocket. Great, that'll keep the fun rolling. But maybe he'll let his guard down and I'll have a chance to grab the gun.

Simon has slipped to the back of the room and is reaching into Mr. Worley's cage. He looks guilty when he sees me watching him, but I wink at him. They're not supposed to mess with Mr. Worley without permission. I think Mrs. Campbell's worried they'll pet all the fur off him—like in *The Velveteen Rabbit*. It's one of their favorite books.

I walk back and pick up Mr. Worley's cage and move it to the floor, motioning for Simon to sit with me. Nick, Tyler, Lewis, and Alicia come over when they see him take Mr. Worley out.

"Mrs. Campbell said we're not supposed to—" Alicia starts out.

"I don't think Mrs. Campbell would mind if we give Mr. Worley a little break from his cage."

Simon holds the hamster like a baby. He buries his face in Mr. Worley's fur. Lewis reaches out for the hamster and Simon pulls away.

"Hold on. You can have a turn next," I tell Lewis.

"He's scared," Simon whispers. "Scared he's gonna die."

I lean down so I can look him straight in the eye. "You tell Mr. Worley that nobody's going to die, okay?"

His big eyes study my face. "But Mr. Worley saw that man shoot Mr. Higgins."

"The security guy? That's his name—Higgins?"

Simon nods.

"Mr. Higgins is fine. I don't think he got hit. He just rolled out of the way."

"Kenji said there was blood in the hall."

"But Mr. Higgins wasn't there," I tell him. "So I think he got up and ran away. You tell Mr. Worley not to worry."

He thinks about that for a minute, then says, "How many lives do we get?"

"What?"

"How many lives do we get after we die?"

"Listen, buddy. You've been playin' too many video games. That is a pretty deep question, and you're gonna have to give me some time to think about it. Here, let's give Lewis a turn."

Lewis reaches out, and I hand off Mr. Worley gently.

Simon looks at me. "I want to go home."

"Soon. We'll get you out of here soon."

"Can Mr. Worley go with me?"

"I don't see why not, if you bring him back tomorrow."

"You mean Monday," Alicia corrects me.

"Oh, yeah. I forgot today's Friday. Do you know what to feed him?"

"Mrs. Campbell gives him lettuce and carrots," Nick says.

"I bet when you get home today, your parents'll be happy to take you to get some lettuce and carrots for Mr. Worley," I tell Simon. I reach over to mess up his hair and say in a silly voice, "Get him some food, Dude!" Our rhyme game pulls a smile from him.

"I know how you can tell if a hamster is a boy or a girl," Alicia announces.

Great. A discussion about the birds and the bees would be dead last on the list of things I want to take on right now.

"The boy hamsters have longer tails."

"Okaaay, that's very interesting," I jump in. "Break time's

over, Mr. Worley, back in your cage." I look up to see Emery trying not to laugh at Alicia's sex ed information. I shrug. Can that be true? Surely Alicia made that up. If there's something sexual about hamster tails, I've never heard it before.

Mr. Worley starts racing like a madman on his wheel the second I put his cage back on the counter.

"He just runs and runs in circles," Nick says, shaking his head.

"Yep. I can relate."

"Ew, look," Tyler squeals and points. Mr. Worley has paused in his race to huddle in a corner and take care of business. They all giggle as poop comes out and drops into the shavings on the floor of the cage. I can't really blame Mr. Worley for having the shit scared out of him.

"Mr. Worley," I tell him, "I feel exactly the same way."

CHAPTER 15

Emery

The clock makes a clicking noise. Eleven o'clock. I glance at the schedule on the wall and turn to Stutts. "I think the kids usually eat now. Do you think we could get them some food?"

"Nobody's coming in, and nobody's going out!" he snarls.

"Okay. Well, some of the kids brought their lunches. Maybe they can share."

"I will," Rose says. "My mama puts too much in, anyway."

"Miss Emery, I have some cupcakes," Simon says quietly, glancing at Stutts.

"That's great. How many do you have, sweetie?"

"A whole bunch. It's my birthday, so my mom sent them."

"Oh, Simon, is it really your birthday? Today?"

He nods solemnly and points at the birthday chart on the wall.

"You didn't even tell us, Pieman," Jake says. "Happy birthday!"

Simon looks down at his feet.

"We'll save them for dessert," I say. I turn to the others. "Maybe all of you could put what you brought on the table to share."

In no time at all the table's heaped high with sandwiches, potato chips, carrot sticks, grapes, fruit bars, cookies, juice boxes—you name it. It's amazing how politely they each pick out something to eat.

"Let's have a picnic on the carpet," I tell them, unwilling to give up the safety of keeping their heads down low. Then something makes me add, "Mr. Jake knows how much I like picnics."

He looks at me and beams. It's the first time I've willingly acknowledged our past.

"Would you like something to eat?" I ask him as I choose several snacks to hand to Patrick.

"No, thanks. Those little bites of food won't do me much good. I need to eat something that recently made noise."

Rose looks up and makes a face.

"Sorry, Rosie," Jake says. "I'm a carnivore. What can I say?"

"Carnivores eat meat," Alicia says.

"We do indeed," he answers.

"Can I pass the cupcakes out?" Simon asks.

"Sure. And I think I saw cups in the cabinet. Maybe we can pour a little from the juice boxes we have so everyone will have something to drink." I look at Stutts, but he ignores me. He's gone quiet again, which is actually even scarier than his manic mode.

Simon goes to the shelf above the cubbies and picks up a cardboard box with a taped-on lid and foil sticking out. He lifts the lid and holds it out to me proudly. Blue icing with sprinkles on top.

"Blue's my favorite color," Simon says.

"They look delicious, sweetheart."

"Happy birthday, Simon," Alicia says, and others chime in.

"Hey, we need to sing," Janita says.

"We don't have any candles." Natalie shakes her head sadly.

"But we can pretend," I tell her, pantomiming putting a candle in a cupcake, lighting a match, holding it to the pretend candle, then handing it to Simon, who watches me, eyes shining. "Can you help me sing the song, Natalie?"

She starts the first few notes and we all join in to sing the birthday song, with Mason Mayfield III ending, predictably, with, "You look like a monkey and you smell like one, too." Simon closes his eyes and blows a soft breath across his cupcake.

"Did you make a wish?" Rose asks shyly.

Simon nods and cuts his eyes at Stutts, who's staring blankly toward the door. His huge shoulders have slumped; his expression is vacant.

I'm wishing, too, Simon.

Simon sets down his cupcake and reaches for two more. Before I can stop him, he marches across the room, hands one to Patrick, and holds the other one out to Stutts, cradling it in outstretched hands like a robin's egg.

It takes the big man a couple of seconds to react. He looks down at the offering and at the trembly smile of its presenter, and his face relaxes just a little.

"Uh, thanks, I'm not hungry."

Simon shrugs and walks slowly back. He replaces the cupcake in the box, then looks at me questioningly, as if wondering if he's done the right thing. I reach over and hug him, my eyes misting at the amazing capacity of kids to respond with love to the chaos around them.

I finish pouring juice and bottled water, then pass out drinks to the kids who don't have their own. "Lefty loosey, righty tighty," I whisper to Lewis, who's struggling with a screw-top plastic juice bottle. He sighs and twists in the opposite direction, popping it open immediately.

"Mason, no cupcake until after lunch."

"Yes, ma'am," he says, lips covered in blue frosting.

"Hey, Emery, can you bring one of those up here?" Jake calls from the computer. He's drifted back up to it while the kids are eating.

"Do I *look* like the pastry waitress?" I ask, but I know he's calling me up for a reason, so I pick up one of the cupcakes and walk over.

Stutts is dividing his attention between the door and the

kids, who are happily chowing down on their shared feast. He takes advantage of the lunch distraction to take several more gulps from his flask.

"Thanks," Jake says, but he barely looks at the cupcake I set next to him. "Hey, take a look at this game I found," he says, kinda loud. "Have you ever played this one before?"

I look at the screen. I can't believe what I'm seeing. We finally have a connection to the outside world and he's on *Facebook* with *Cole*?

"I think the best strategy," Jake says in a chatty tone, "is to hold down the button while you aim the grenade."

I keep my expression normal while whispering through gritted teeth, "Really, Jake? You're talking to *Cole*?"

Stutts doesn't seem concerned with us right now, and the kids are getting louder while they eat, so we take this opportunity to argue under our breaths.

"What have you got against Cole?"

"Other than the fact that he's an insensitive racist misogynist? Nothing."

"Why do you say that?"

"You've seen how he treats girls. Jake, we need help. How can you chat with Cole when we're in terrible danger?"

"Read it, Emery. I went through him to get help from the police."

The word *police* rings out through a lull in the kids' conversations and I freeze. I don't dare look at Stutts, but my entire body radiates fear as I wait for his reaction. The seconds drag by and the kids go back to their chatter. I start breathing again and scroll backward to read Jake's chat with Cole (and our principal, it turns out).

"See, you have to hit this target first," Jake says out loud, giving me time to read. "It's kind of like that other game we used to play. What was the name of that game? It was back in middle school and I can't think of what it was called, but we played it all the time." He's rambling and I offer some vague answer.

Just as I get to the end, the chat screen pops up again and Cole is there. Or maybe it's Mr. Chapman.

jake u there?

that you, cole?

yep. chief said tell you theyre talking to the wife, her names silda, to see if she can talk him down.

There's more, but I can't read the rest. Alarm bells are going off in my head and an icy chill runs down my back. I grab Jake's arm. *Silda.* He said *Silda.* Stutts's wife's name is Silda!

"Jake," I whisper frantically. "I know her!"

"Who?" he asks.

"Silda." I drop my voice, and Jake leans in to hear me. "That's Molly's cousin, the one with the crazy husband who tried to kill her. Oh God, Brian Stutts must be the husband, the one she called the cops on when he beat her up!"

Jake's looking at me like I'm speaking Swahili.

"I can't believe Molly's related to Patrick and I never knew it. Oh, Jake, I've heard terrible stories about this guy!"

CHAPTER 16

JAKE

EMERY'S STARING AT THE SCREEN, her eyes wide.

"Wait, Molly's cousin is Patrick's mom? You know her?" I'm having trouble keeping up.

"I've never met her. They just moved back here last year." Emery looks over at Stutts, but the kids are too loud for him to hear us talking this low. "He went crazy and attacked her while she was asleep. She woke up with his hands around her throat. She realized he was still asleep and started fighting him, but before she could wake him up, he punched her in the face and broke her cheekbone."

"This is crazy. You're sure it was him?" I ask.

"How many Sildas can there be? Especially ones with a husband home from Iraq? It's him, all right. Molly said the police took him away in handcuffs. He was crying and yelling and just basically off his rocker. She said he has PTSD—post-traumatic stress disorder. He can't handle being back home after being in Iraq. Or maybe he can't handle the things he did in Iraq, I don't know."

"What else did she say about him?"

"I'm trying to remember. I wasn't paying that much attention because I didn't know it would be important."

I reach for the keyboard again.

cole, can you get molly? emery thinks stutts's wife is her cousin.

no shit. sure, i'll send somebody. do you know where she is?

Emery looks at the clock and thinks for a few seconds. "Chemistry," she says, so I type it in.

A phone rings in Stutts's pocket, and he takes it out and looks at it. He makes a face, then puts it back and goes back to watching the door.

"And you can get bonus points here," I say in a normal voice to Emery, pointing at the screen.

"I remember now," she says. "You can't move to the next level until you finish off all these guys."

We make up more crap about the pretend game, but Stutts doesn't look our way again. Then another line appears on the screen.

Emery, are you there? Its Molly. OMG, are you ok?

"Your turn," I say out loud to Emery, sliding over for her to take the keyboard. "Let's see if you can catch up, worthy opponent."

Hey Mols. We're ok, but I need you to tell me and Jake about Silda's husband. He's holding us hostage.

Brian? I cant believe it! Cole said he shot somebody.

A security guard. Don't know if he's ok or not.

Oh, Emery, be careful, hes crazy.

I know you said he has PTSD. I can't remember what else you said.

He was ok when he first came home. And he used to be great guy. Pres of his class at high school and capt of football team. Silda said it started with nightmares and he was really moody and started drinking. She took Patrick and left.

Drinking now.

Hes messed up. He wont even sit with his back to doors at restaurants and at her little brothers ball game he made her wait til everbody left gym before he did.

???

He always thinks somebodys after him. He watches roofs of buildings for snipers. She said its like his bodys overly tuned to danger and cant turn off. He takes a gun everywhere. She was afraid Patrick would mess with it.

Can't believe Patrick's your cousin and I never made the connection. He's so adorable.

No reasn for you to. Hes a sweet kid.

What else do you know?

He threw a bottle at a wall after she found him passed out at lunch one day. and I remember he had a panic atack in the grocery store.

Did she try to get him to go for help?

He wouldnt. He said if you admit you have problem, your army career is over. Nobdy wants to be in life-or-death situation with somebody whos messed up.

You told me he broke her cheekbone?

Yeah, she called cops and they took him to jail but she dropped the charges cuz she didnt want to lock up

Patricks dad. but she filed for dvorce and full custody.
Doesnt trust him with Patrick. Emery, be careful,
sweetie. Im so worried about yall.

We will. Gotta go. Hey, Mols, will you call my mom?

Sure, Em. and tell her what?

Tell her I'm ok and I love her.

"Take that, Willoughby," Emery says, fake-gloating loudly with a glance at Stutts, while I close the screen. I notice her hand shaking on the keyboard and I lay mine on top of it for just a minute and squeeze her fingers. She squeezes mine back.

CHAPTER 17
Emery

Jake's hand over my shaking fingers is the only thing keeping me from coming unglued right now. I know he can tell how freaked out I am now that I know who Stutts is, but I'm proud of myself for ignoring the POTS monster right now. I can't let my symptoms keep me from helping these kids. I glance over at Silda's violent husband, and he's gone back to staring off into space, his hand resting on the table next to Patrick, tapping the butt of the gun against the wood—like a *tick-tick-tick*ing bomb about detonate.

We're running out of time. We've got to get these kids out of here.

Suddenly, the intercom crackles, making all of us jump.

"Mr. Stutts, this is Chief Reed Walker with HPD. We want to resolve this situation as quickly as possible so the children can be released. We want to talk with you about your demands privately—"

"No!" Stutts yells, jumping to his feet. "No one's coming in here. Do you hear me?"

"Mr. Stutts, we need to talk with you about what you want. Your wife gave us the number to your cell phone, and we want to—"

"You leave her out of this!" Stutts screams. "What I *want* is to walk out of here with my son. There's nothing to talk about. You people just want to take my son away from me."

"Mr. Stutts, if we could just—"

"Shut up! Don't talk to me! Just shut up!" He's shouting at the intercom box like a maniac, and my heart sinks. Nothing good can come of getting him all riled up.

"Why don't you let—" the voice continues.

Stutts raises his arm and there's a loud blast—a deafening *KA-BOOM*—that rocks the room. The intercom box shatters and splinters of wood fly out from the wall. A couple of kids scream.

"Get down!" I yell, diving from the computer toward where the kids are sitting on the floor. The gun blast seems to reverberate through the room. I shove the ones nearest me to get their heads down, and the others duck, too.

Jake is there beside me, putting himself between Stutts and us. Stutts wheels around and yells at the crying children, "Shut up! All of you!" My heart stops as he points at Jake with the gun. "You get them quiet."

We try to shush the children, but it's no use. They've had about all the trauma they can stand.

"I said quiet!" Stutts says. "Make them stop."

"We're doing the best we can," Jake says, exasperated. "They're scared."

"Mr. Stutts, if you could just give us a minute to . . ." My voice is shaking, and it sounds far away through the ringing in my ears.

"Shut up, shut up! Just shut the hell up—all of you!" His face is deep red.

"You've got to cut these kids some slack," Jake says, standing up to face the crazy man with the smoking gun—which scares me to death. "Look at them. They're not built for this kind of stress, man. If you could let some of them go . . ."

The kids are pitiful. They're huddled together, and most are sobbing—some at top volume.

"Don't tell me what to do." Stutts takes a step toward Jake. I cringe, but Jake doesn't flinch; he keeps talking in a low, steady voice. *Jake, don't do this.*

"Mr. Stutts, keep me," he continues. He's using all his powers of persuasion, and Jake has many, I can tell you. "My dad's the mayor. People do what he says. Use me to get what you want. Just let the kids go."

Stutts glares at him for what seems like an hour, then snarls suddenly, "Some of them."

"What?" His unexpected answer throws Jake for a second.

"Just some of them. Get the loud ones out of here, so I can think." He reaches up and rubs his forehead. "Now."

Oh my God! He's letting the kids go! I can't believe it!

"But make it fast," Stutts orders.

"Hey, guys, it's okay." I swing into action before he can change his mind. "You can get up now. I need you to line up, very quietly, starting right here by me."

Immediately there's chaos as they stumble toward the door, pushing and shoving. "Me, me!" "I want to go home!" "Me first!"

"Anyone who's making a sound," I yell above the noise, "won't be allowed to go." Silence. God bless Willa Campbell—best teacher role model ever. The kids line up without speaking. Several are dragging backpacks.

"Leave your things here," I tell them. "You can get them tomorrow, okay?"

"Can I get my snack?" Mason asks.

"I promise, your parents will feed you all the snacks you want when you get home."

"But what about our take-home folders?" Alicia asks.

"Later," I practically yell at her. "We need to move quickly."

Before the unpredictable Mr. Stutts takes back his offer.

I look at the small faces turned hopefully in my direction. "Okay, three at a time from the front of the line. Tyler and Janita and Olivia, you're first. Mr. Stutts, I'm sending these three out now."

"Hold up a sec," Jake says.

He moves to the door and raises his voice. "We're sending some of the kids out. Can you hear me? Some of the students are coming out into the hallway." He doesn't add "Don't shoot them," but we're all thinking it.

"Go ahead," a deep voice answers. "Tell them to walk slowly."

To the kids I say, "Just walk very slowly down the hall and turn left toward the office. Someone will be there to take you to your parents."

"Miss Emery, are you coming with us?" Janita asks, grabbing my hand.

"Not now, but we won't be too far behind you," I tell her.

"Are you gonna be okay?" she asks tearfully.

"Don't you worry. We'll be fine." I squeeze her hand.

Olivia reaches up to hug me.

"I'll see you soon, Livie. I promise."

She nods, sniffling, and I usher them into the hallway. I push them forward and they waddle like baby ducks in a row down the hall. I can hear people talking to them as they turn the corner.

"Okay, next three . . ." I turn to the line. "Mason, Kimberly, and Anna-Caroline." Stutts doesn't move or say a word. Patrick stays seated. Kenji has come to the front of the room to stand next to him, his hand on Patrick's shoulder.

"Later, Gator," Mason Mayfield III says, pointing at Jake.

"No talking." Jake shakes his head at Mason, who makes an *oops* face and pantomimes a *zip your lip* motion.

"Three more coming out," Jake calls out into the hall.

"Okay, ready," comes the answer.

They move into the hallway—out of danger, thank God—without incident, and I line up three more. "Nick, Kaela, and Abbey."

Relief washes over me with each group that leaves— three more kids out of Stutts's reach. After the tension of the morning, I have an insane urge to hug Stutts for this small concession. And I could kiss Jake for making it happen. Damn, I must be really tired.

Jake and I feed DeQuan, Lewis, and Carlos into the hallway. Then there are only six kids left, including Patrick.

"That's it," Stutts barks suddenly. "The rest stay."

"But, Mr. Stutts, there are only a few more. You can keep me and Jake." I can't even look at the disappointed faces of the kids who are left—watching their friends leave and knowing they can't.

"No!" Stutts bellows. "I'm not giving up all of them!"

The kids left behind—Patrick, Kenji, Simon, Rose, Natalie, and Alicia—are quiet, except for Natalie, who immediately goes into full-on drama-queen mode. "I want my daddy! I want my momma! I want to go home!"

"Shh, Natalie." I lean down and pull her to me.

Natalie sobs louder. "I want Gran. I want Pop, and Buffy, and Socks."

I look up at Stutts, my eyebrows raised in a question.

"Get her out of here," he says roughly.

Jake calls "One more" out the door, and we usher Natalie, still wailing, through it. Her loud sobs can be heard growing fainter as she reaches the corner and turns into the office hall.

Stutts looks around at the rest of us. Rose walks toward Jake and reaches up to hang on his arm. Kenji remains with Patrick. Simon sits quietly nearby, staring owl-eyed at our little tableau; Mrs. C. calls him her "old soul." Alicia looks up expectantly at me, waiting for directions I can't give her. No one knows what happens next.

"How many children are left with you?" a voice calls down the hall.

"Five. We have five," I answer, looking to make sure I'm right. It's hard to think straight.

"Mr. Stutts, please release all the children," the voice calls out. "We can talk about what you want when all the children have been sent out."

"Tell him no way," Stutts says to me. "I'm not talking to anybody."

Not sure how I've become the translator, I call out through the door, "Mr. Stutts says he's keeping these five. Jake and I are here with them. We'll take care of them." I look over at Jake. He nods, and I realize we're a team.

"Do you need anything?" the voice says. "Will he let us send in some food?"

Stutts shakes his head.

"We're okay for now," I call out.

"Get back from that door," Stutts orders.

The room seems empty with two-thirds of the kids gone. I try to rally, smiling at the unlucky ones and herding them back to the carpet again, all except Patrick, who stays where he is. They gather in a tight little group, with not one word of complaint, sweet angels. I'm almost sure I catch a faint whiff of Mrs. Campbell's perfume, and I close my eyes, wishing we had her back.

Rose must have noticed it, too. "Can we sing a song?" she asks. "Mrs. Campbell always says singing makes you feel better."

"Sure," I answer. "What would you like to sing?"

"I know, we can sing 'The Wheels on the Bus,'" Alicia says.

"That's a baby song," Rose complains.

"Okay, then, 'John Jacob Jingleheimer Schmidt,'" Alicia says.

"What else do you know?" I ask.

"How 'bout 'Edelweiss'?" Simon asks.

"Y'all know 'Edelweiss'?" I ask, the word catching in my throat. My dad used to sing it when he rocked me to sleep.

"It's Mrs. Campbell's favorite. She let us watch *The Sound of Music*," Rose says.

"Twice," Simon says.

"Mrs. Campbell taught us the words. She said it's a flower," Alicia says.

Rose settles it, starting out on her own. "Edelweiss, edelweiss." The others join in—Alicia confidently, Kenji quietly, and Simon with his serious intensity. The spontaneous song makes me ache; they're so brave and sincere, singing their little hearts out with an armed gunman ten feet away.

As the notes float upward, a wave of memories of my father rolls over me, and I feel a sob bubble up in my chest.

After the first few lines, the children stall, stuck for the words. There's a moment of dead air time, and I look helplessly at Jake and shake my head, teary-eyed, unable to make a sound without totally falling apart. Jake shrugs. He doesn't know the words and I can't sing them right now. The children lapse into silence.

Suddenly, out of nowhere, the air is filled with the melody of a sweet, high voice from the front of the room—so pure it sends a shiver through me.

Patrick!

His head is raised; the words are strong and clear. All of us look up in surprise as he fills in the missing words.

"Blossom of snow, may you bloom and grow, bloom and grow forever."

His voice is haunting, and his face is filled with an angelic light. He seems unaware that anyone else is in the room; he's caught up in the melody and transported to some place far away. He holds every note a little long before releasing it, as if it's hard to part with each fragile bit of the melody.

"E-del-weiss, e-del-weiss, bless our homeland for-e-ver."

The last clear note surrounds us. He stops and the room is silent, electrified by the unexpected solo. No one moves. The air is filled with the beauty of the simple melody and the power of his small voice.

-Then Patrick realizes we're staring, transfixed. He looks down at his hands in his lap and I see a tear drop onto his tiny thumb.

His father gazes toward the back windows without moving. His eyes are unfocused and distant.

"Patrick, that was beautiful," I manage to whisper.

He looks up at me, and his lower lip trembles. "I want my mama," he says in a desperate whisper, another tear slipping down his cheek as his face collapses in a sob.

I kneel beside his chair and hold him, refusing to look at his father, smoothing his hair and speaking softly to him while he cries. I feel so guilty for all the comfort we've given the others. This child needed me, too, but he was denied my help because of my fear. His small body melts into my side and his head rests on my shoulder as he clings to me. The other children watch in respectful silence until his cries taper off to whimpers. Eventually, a soft tick from the clock is the only sound in the room.

I never knew. In all the times I heard him hum to himself, in all the times I coaxed him to speak, I never saw this kind of confidence. Music brought strength from a place deep inside him that *no one* can touch.

Stutts stands and moves toward me. I stiffen. Then he reaches out and puts his hand on his son's shoulder. His jaw clenches and his Adam's apple moves in a hard swallow. Patrick remains motionless and we stand there, the three of us, linked by bizarre circumstance and uncertain fate.

Eventually, I hear a soft yawn behind me and turn to see Rose's head nodding.

The clock says 11:45. It feels like we've been in this room for days. The schedule on the wall shows 12:00–12:20 as Rest Time.

"What do y'all do during Rest Time?" I ask Simon.

"We put our heads down on our desks and listen to music or nature sounds."

"Okay with you?" I ask Stutts. "I think they're used to a break now."

He doesn't answer at first. Then he nods.

"I'll get our pillows out," Kenji says, running to a large shelf in back.

"Can we listen to the ocean?" Rose asks. They're eager for routine.

"It's over here. On this tape." Alicia points to an old boom box. "It has seagulls, too."

"A big yes to seagulls," Jake says, moving to help Kenji with the pillows.

I place Patrick gently in the chair near his dad and give him a squeeze before letting go. He watches as the others settle in.

"Can Patrick sit with us?" Kenji asks, looking at his friend across the room.

"Patrick's okay, honey."

"Here's his pillow." Kenji hands it to me. I smile at Patrick and toss it to him. He looks pleased as he hugs it to his chest.

"Thanks, Kenji. You're a good friend," I tell him.

Patrick holds out Lamby, and Rose looks up at me. I nod and she runs to the front of the room to retrieve her stuffed animal for nap time, then returns, rubbing him against her face.

Simon reaches over and slips his small hand in mine as I pull a chair up beside him.

"What happened here?" I ask, touching the blister on his palm.

"Monkey bars," he says.

"Can I sit in your lap—just for a minute?" Rose whispers.

I shift position and pat my legs. Her face lights up and she climbs onto my lap, curling against me with her head burrowed into my shoulder. I wrap my arms around her and turn a little so I have a better view of Stutts and Patrick. I make eye contact with Patrick across the room, and he lays his head on his pillow.

The kids are slow to settle down, except Patrick, who's asleep almost immediately. Jake's gone back to the computer. I look over at the top of his head, just visible above the monitor, and try to remind myself why I used to hate him.

Even though they don't all sleep, their eyes are closed, so there's no one to see the tears that roll down my face and drop onto the top of Rose's head. She doesn't notice, and I'm able to stop the flow before the waterworks get out of hand.

I can't let my guard down. I have to hold it together for the kids.

It's going to be all right, I tell myself. *Everyone's going to walk out of here today. We're all going to be fine.*

Everything will be okay. It has to be.

"Miss Emery?" Rose looks up. "Are you okay?" She pats my arm protectively.

And I realize I'm shaking—hard.

CHAPTER 18

JAKE

I STARE AT THE COMPUTER SCREEN.

When examined, female hamsters
have their anal and genital open-
ings close together, whereas males
have these two holes farther apart
(the penis is usually withdrawn into
the coat and thus appears as a hole
or pink pimple).

Okay, I admit it; I had to look it up. I'm a Wiki-
pedia nerd. I knew Alicia'd made that up about the
boy hamster's tail being longer. But sometimes
when these kids say something crazy, it turns out
they're right. It was gonna bug me until I checked
it out.

Poor little hamster guy. A penis that looks like

a pimple? Man, *that* would be depressing. I click to another site to double check.

Wait a minute. There it is. Unbelievable! Crap, Alicia wins again.

> The back end of the male tends to be elongated and rounder in appearance in comparison to the female.

I'll be damned. She must have heard somebody say that and misunderstood *tail*? Or maybe I misunderstood *tail*? Hell, I must be losing it. Researching hamster sex is probably not the best use of my time right now. I open Facebook and Cole is there.

> *molly told me about the dude. scary shit. guys not playin with full deck*

> *f'real*

> *hold on. chaps back. wants to talk to you*

> *Jake, Mr. Chapman here. Chief Walker wants you to describe the room and tell us exactly where the gunman is sitting.*

> *stutts, his name is stutts.*

Mr. Stutts, sorry.

hold on a minute. i have an idea.

I shut down Facebook and reach for Mrs. Campbell's cell phone. I gotta be a fool to try to take a picture right now, but if it would help them see where everybody is in the room . . . I don't even want to think about them rushing the guy, but if that's what they're planning, I sure as hell want it to go well. If I can prop the phone between the two stacks of books on Mrs. Campbell's desk, maybe I can pull it off.

The ocean tape Emery's playing for the kids is getting to Stutts. Even though he hasn't taken his eyes off the door, he's kinda spaced-out looking. He's leaning his head back against the wall, but his eyes are open.

I'm pretty wiped out, too. My buddy Hunter, who's a little obsessive sometimes, told me once that when he's on an airplane, he holds his feet up a few inches off the floor the whole time 'cause he's convinced the plane'll crash if he puts them down. Well, that's how I feel—like I've been holding an airplane in the sky all day.

I click on the camera icon, then glance up at Stutts. He's not looking. I prop the phone on the desk, just to the right of the stack of books, checking the screen to get as much of the room in the photo as possible. The position's too low to get a good view. I slide another book underneath. My left arm is hidden behind the books, but I keep my right hand on the keyboard and my eyes on the screen so it'll still look like I'm playing a game.

I hold my breath and snap the picture. Stutts looks over at me. My body tenses and my heart misfires. Shit! I'm not sure what he'll do if he catches me, but if past experience is any gauge, he tends to shoot when he's mad.

I lay the phone flat and put both hands on the computer keys. I can feel his eyes on me as I stare at the screen and type random keys.

"What are you doing?" he yells at me.

I look up innocently. I rest my hands on the keyboard to keep them from shaking.

"Nothing—just moving a book out of the way." My voice sounds high even to me.

He stares at me and squints his eyes.

"It was about to fall off the desk." I turn away like nothing's going on and focus on the screen.

Let it go, let it go, don't come over here, please don't come over here.

"Mr. Stutts, could we turn out the lights?" Emery asks, drawing his attention from me. I'm not sure if she's doing it on purpose, but it was most excellent timing. "Maybe just the switch for the back?"

To my surprise, he stands up and flips the switch, leaving the back half of the room a little darker.

He goes back to his chair, and I pretend I'm playing the game. I don't dare look over to see if he's looking. Time passes and he seems to have forgotten me, thank God.

After a little while longer, I reach for the phone and slide it toward me. I click on the photo. Damn, Willoughby, you oughta be a private eye. You can't see all the kids, but Stutts's position in the room is clear in relation to the door. I'm not sure how much this will help them, but if Stutts goes crazy and starts shooting, they'll know where he is, at least for now. Stutts shooting—shit, I have to make sure that doesn't happen.

I click the message button and send it to Cole's phone.

Stutts leans back in his chair again, focused on the door. I open Facebook again and look for Cole.

Cole: check yr phone. but tell them not to do anything yet. give us time to talk to him now that most kids are gone. maybe we can get him to let others go. ill check back when i can.

I close chat and go back to games. I lean back in my chair and yawn and stretch. I swear I should get an Oscar. It's starting to wear me out—pretending not to be scared outta my mind.

I learned to be a pretty good actor when my mom died. The whole time I was standing next to her coffin in my new suit, shaking hands with people, I was just thinking, "I want my momma," over and over again like a little kid.

CHAPTER 19

Emery

Simon's snoring quietly; he's out. I give Rose a hug and slide her onto my chair. Alicia's breathing evenly, her small hand under her freckled cheek.

I walk to the back of the room and get three Diet Cokes from Mrs. C's fridge. I put one in front of Jake, then take a deep breath, walk to the front, and hold one out to Stutts. He eyes me warily, then reaches for the can.

I pull up a chair beside him—not too close. Without speaking, I look back at the sleeping children. I feel Stutts watching me—and Jake watching us from the computer.

My heart's racing. Maybe Jake's right and I'm making a mistake, but I have to try. Any kind of connection I can make with Stutts could make a difference for us if things fall apart here. We can't just sit and wait to see what happens. No matter how this goes, I have to know when it's all over that I did everything I could to help these kids, to help Stutts see us as people instead of targets.

Stutts doesn't say anything, just looks back at the door. Then, so quietly I almost don't hear him, he says, "How long do they rest?"

It's a start. "Um, the schedule says twenty minutes. We're not usually here this time of day."

He glances up at the clock.

I lean forward a little. "Were there a lot of kids over there—in Iraq?" I ask.

He doesn't answer at first. Then: "Yeah."

"Did you have much contact with them?"

He waits, like he's deciding whether to tell me to get lost, then says, "They ran beside our vehicles, begging."

"For food?"

"Candy . . . sometimes money. We had to stop giving them stuff because they'd run out in the road. And if you gave something to one kid, another one would beat him up for it."

"Were they hungry?"

"Some of them. There were packs that ran together . . . dirty . . . barefoot."

"Where were their parents?"

He pauses. "Some didn't have any—orphans of the war. The ones who did—I don't know. Sometimes schools were damaged in the bombing; I guess if the school was closed, the parents didn't have anything to do with the kids while they worked, so they just ran wild."

"Did they speak English?"

A rare half smile; for the first time I see how much he looks like Patrick. "Things like 'give me' and 'USA.' My buddy Tucker taught them some English."

"Is he back home—your buddy?"

"Tucker? Yeah, he's back."

"Do you talk to him much?"

"No, Tucker's not doing too great," he says. "What people don't understand is, you can't ever go home. You pretend you can pick up where you left off, but you're not the same person." He looks around the room. "It'd be like you trying to go back to elementary school again. You think you could fit in here if you tried hard enough?"

I glance over at the kids and shake my head.

"War changes you," he says. "You know things you didn't before." He frowns. "It takes something from you that you never get back. One day you're pickin' pieces of brain matter off your shirt from the guy who was sitting next to you, and a few weeks later—back at home—you're supposed to get all worked up over whether the city's gonna fix the potholes on Jefferson Street. Everybody wants to talk to you about gas prices or who's gonna win the football game. Who gives a shit, man? People are dying all over the world."

He shakes his head in disgust. "People see homeless veterans sleeping in the streets and they just turn away. They don't care what happens to you after you get back. They don't get it that you can't sleep in a bed. Can't be part of a family. Can't be part of a community."

His eyes darken. "You think you'll appreciate life when you get back, but the sad truth is, you miss death, at least the fear of it. It's like you can't see what's good in the world around you without the constant reminder that you can lose it all. You come home and realize you've turned into an adrenaline junkie. You crave the high, you need the drama. Civilian life doesn't do it for you anymore."

His words are coming faster now. "You're surrounded by death every minute over there. You don't wait for death to come for you; you have to go out every day looking for it. I used to pray not to die, first few weeks I was over there. I'd picture my kid at my funeral, and I'd pray I'd make it back home to watch him grow up. And then I'd have dreams that my legs were blown off, and I prayed I *would* die—if it meant not being a cripple for life. And then I saw a guy get burned up in a Humvee, and I started praying to die quickly if I had to go—a clean shot to the head. You get to where you don't know what to pray for."

He looks me in the eyes. "People don't know what really matters."

It's the most I've heard him say—and the calmest he's been.

Maybe it's a little peek into what he was like before.

"What really matters to you?" I ask.

"My kid. My wife." His voice cracks a little on the word *wife* and he looks away. "My country. In that order."

"How long have you been back?"

"Eight months." He looks over at Patrick. "While I was

there, I couldn't think of anything else but being back with my family. The pictures Silda sent of Patrick were what kept me going. But then when I got home, I couldn't make it work."

My heart races at the mention of Silda's name.

"You can't understand, unless you've lived for months in the middle of people trying to kill you. You live in constant fear, always on your guard because if you're not hyperaware, you're dead." He leans toward me, his breath reeking of alcohol. "Not dead like in some fucking video game. Dead dead. Turned to pink mist, they call it."

"Can't the army help you," I ask, "to readjust to normal life?"

"Normal," he grunts. "What the hell is normal? Oh yeah, they help you get ready to go home, all right. You know what the army calls reintegration? Some lame video they make you watch while everybody's dog tired and half asleep. It's a big joke.

"Yeah, people like you think you want to know all about it, but you don't really want to hear about the stench of gore, the smell of charred bodies in the street—*pieces* of *people*. I don't know which is worse—looking at that shit when you first get there because the sick part of you wants to know what it looks like, or later on when you don't look at it because you've seen it all before. Stuff that's so bad, it can't be said out loud. Unspeakable, that's what it is."

I shiver in the warm room.

"Listen." He looks in my eyes. I want to pull away from him, but I don't. "Once you've pulled that trigger—once you watch a man die and you know you killed him—you're never the same. You can tell yourself he was gonna kill you first. You can say over and over again that he was the enemy. But he's still a guy just fighting for what he believes in— maybe a guy who's a lot like you—and his life is over, done. His wife's got no husband, his kid's got no daddy. Why? Because you killed him—that's why."

He lapses into silence. The room is quiet except for Mr. Worley's wheel creaking from the back of the room over the sound of Simon's soft snoring.

"You start seeing him," he finally continues, "that guy you killed, and you wonder if his ghost can find you. Is he watching you while you brush your teeth, while you eat your breakfast? Is he waiting for a chance to fuck you up?"

Suddenly he looks over at Jake at the computer and barks, "Hey! You better be playing video games!"

Patrick jumps in his sleep at the sound.

Jake looks up and holds up both hands. "Tetris, man. Come look. I'm just keeping busy over here. Trying to stay out of your hair."

Stutts stares hard at Jake for about ten seconds.

"How long were you in Iraq?" I ask, trying to get him to talk again. But the mood is broken.

"Look, I don't want to—"

And then, without warning, all hell breaks loose.

A bright light flashes above the door and a horrendously loud buzzing sound fills the room. I look up in confusion as Stutts yells above the noise.

"What the hell's going on? What are they trying to pull?"

It's the fire alarm!

The kids sit up and look around, dazed. Several cover their ears with their hands. A couple of them stand up. They're conditioned to respond, but when they look for the teacher to find out what to do, they remember she's not here. And I don't have a clue.

Stutts is freaking out. "It's a trick. Nobody's leaving. Shut that thing off. Shut it off! Now!" He's yelling above the horrible racket.

"It's okay," I yell back. "We're not leaving." Jake moves toward the kids, and I hurry back to help him reassure them.

"It's probably a false alarm," I shout above the din. "Surely they'll shut it off."

And then, thankfully, the noise stops.

"We're supposed to go outside," Alicia says.

Jake shushes her, holding up a finger and cocking his head. "Wait a minute. Listen."

In the sudden silence, we can hear the all-call intercom announcement from the hallway—even though our intercom box is blown to smithereens. We have to listen hard to decipher it.

"Teachers, please disregard the fire alarm. Do *not* leave your classrooms. This is a false alarm. We neglected to disable it for our once-a-month practice fire drill. Again, I repeat, do *not* leave your classrooms."

Great! *This* is *a drill; this is* not *a drill.* If we weren't confused before, we certainly are now. We've got a crazy guy with an itchy trigger finger, and they can't remember to turn the fire alarm off. And these are the people I'm supposed to have confidence in to help us. I already felt like we were on our own here; now I know we are.

Stutts goes to the door and yells without putting his head out. "You people better keep that thing off. Don't pull another stunt like that with me."

Suddenly there's an eerie noise from the back of the classroom, and we all turn toward the sound. It's Simon— wailing for all he's worth. The shock of waking up to such chaos has finally been the last straw, poor guy. He's crying pitiful chest-heaving sobs, gulping and gasping for breath between cries.

Jake bends down and puts his arm around Simon's shoulders, talking quietly to him, so I turn to the other kids. "It's okay, y'all. Try to rest a little longer. It was just a false alarm. Everything's okay."

I feel like a recording—the kind you get when you call a business, the kind that doesn't really say anything but just keeps you holding on with promises of a real person, a grown-up, to help solve your problem.

But the longer we wait here together, the more it starts to feel like help will never come. My reassurances to the kids sound fake—even to me.

CHAPTER 20

JAKE

AWESOME. THE ONLY THING WE WERE missing in this entire shit-storm of a day was a fake fire drill. Now my life is complete.

"It's okay, dude," I yell above Simon's sobbing; he is in the middle of a balls-to-the-wall meltdown. "Look, no fire. No problems. It's all good, man."

He keeps up the noise, his howling blending with the echo of the fire alarm in my ears. What, were they trying to turn that thing up loud enough for the deaf kids to hear it?

"Everything's okay, buddy. Uncle Jake's on duty," I tell him. Kenji has come over to Simon's desk and he's patting him on the shoulder.

Man, I feel for the little guy. I've been there. You're in that really deep sleep and something wakes you up and you can't figure out where the hell you are and then you remember something really terrible that happened to you that you forgot for just a little while . . . like your mom dying.

My mom died at three thirty in the morning, and for about three weeks after that, I'd wake up at three thirty every morning. It was weird. I'd be sound asleep—and then I wasn't. And I knew without looking at the clock what time it was. It was like my subconscious was trying to warn me that something really bad happens at that time.

I pat Simon on the head and give Emery a helpless face so she'll rescue me. Comforting hysterical kids is not part of my skill set. She comes over, sits beside him, and hugs him. He starts to quiet down as soon as she whispers to him, thank God.

Stutts goes back to his seat watching the door, but he looks majorly pissed—not a good sign. It takes Emery and me about ten minutes to quiet the kids down again. Amazingly, Kenji and Rose seem ready to go back to resting; their little brains must be worn out from all the crap they've put up with in the past few hours. Alicia keeps her head down, but she opens her eyes every now and then to make sure we're still here. Simon joins the others, still sniffling, and eventually falls back asleep.

The truth is, I needed a break from playing cops and robbers with the local police on the computer, so the false alarm wasn't all bad. I walk over to where Emery's sitting. Her eyes have a faraway look and she's twirling the piece of hair she always tugs on. I reach down and hold her fingers to stop her and she blushes. It's nice to feel like I can touch her again without her pulling away.

"Sorry," she says. "I don't even know I'm doing it."

"No problem," I say. "I just don't want you to wear all the shine off."

She smiles.

I take her hand and pull her from her seat, motioning for her to join me in the back of the room. We sit on the floor, far enough from Stutts to talk with the ocean noise covering us, and lean against the wall. Stutts watches but doesn't object.

"I sent a picture of the room to the cops," I whisper below the seagull sounds.

"For what?"

"I dunno. In case they have to come in."

"You mean, like, with guns? God, I hope that doesn't happen."

"If they don't, how does this end?" I look her straight in the eye.

She shakes her head. "Maybe we can talk to him," she says. "Get him to turn himself in. He has to know by now it's his only choice."

"Not his only choice."

She looks at me like I've slapped her. Surely to God she's thought through the possibilities.

"You don't think he'd . . . ?"

"I don't know whether he'd hurt the kids. He might. But I think it's more likely he'd hurt himself."

She looks stunned. "Oh no, he can't do that. Not with Patrick . . ."

"I hope not, Em. I'm just sayin' . . ."

"Jake, I saw a SWAT team suiting up outside," she whispers, "and there were ambulances. You don't think the cops'd shoot into a room with kids inside, do you?"

"Not unless they had to—but we don't know what he'll do. And Emery, you're not gonna get anywhere trying to talk to him," I tell her. "So just stay away from him, okay? There's no way to know what will set him off."

"Are you implying that I'll say the wrong thing? I'm not stupid, you know."

"Oh God, Em, I know you're not stupid. You're—hell, you're the smartest person I know. That's not what I meant."

"Why can't you just trust me a little?" she fires back at me. "That's something you don't know much about, Jake—trust."

"There it is. Jesus, just shoot me!" I yell at her, frustrated that she's back on *that* again.

I don't even realize what I've said at first.

Emery's staring at me in horror, Stutts glares at me, and Alicia sits up, her eyes on the gun in Stutts's hand.

I am *such* a moron. I can't believe I just said that. "Sorry, bad timing," I say, holding up my hands in surrender. "I didn't mean it."

Stutts leans forward in his seat, looking at us like he's about to tell us not to talk, then changes his mind and sits back.

I turn back to Emery and lower my voice. "Emery, you have to believe me. *You* are the only girl I've ever really cared about."

"You should have thought about that when you were all over Stacey Jordan!" she snaps.

"It wasn't what you think. The whole thing got blown out of proportion."

"I can't do this right now," Emery says, moving away from me. "There are more important things to deal with."

I grab her arm. "I know, I messed up. Sometimes my brain just takes a vacation."

She pulls away from me. "Did you even read the note I wrote you?" I ask. "I meant everything I said about wanting you back."

"Can we *please* change the *subject?*" she says.

Rose whimpers like a puppy; we look over, but she's asleep. I can feel Emery breathing deep beside me to calm down.

"Truce, Jake. We gotta work together here," she says. "This isn't about us. It's about them." Then, for the first time, she sounds unsure of herself. "I was just trying to make a connection with Stutts. It seemed like a good idea."

"What was he talking about?" I ask, trying to play nice again.

"Just how hard it is to come back home, how boring ordinary life is."

"So he decided to hold up a first grade classroom for fun?"

"He's scared, Jake. Scared of losing everything. He's lost his wife and now she's trying to take his son away. That's what this is all about—she's trying to get full custody of Patrick."

"Well, he picked a shitty way to do it. If she didn't have what she needed to take Patrick away before, she's got it now."

"I think he knows that. I don't think he ever intended for this to happen. The situation just got out of control before he could stop it."

She looks me in the eye. "Don't you ever wish you could rewind something you've done that turned out to be so much worse than you thought?" she asks, but this time she looks more sad than angry.

I think for a minute about the best way to answer, and then I just say, "Yeah."

She glances at Stutts. "I don't think he . . ." She stops, like she's figuring out what it's like for him.

"What?"

"I don't think he has complete control of his actions. And that's what scares me. He does things without thinking."

"Like the security guard."

"Yeah, he just reacted instinctively," she says.

"And his instinct is to shoot."

"Jake, if he has post-traumatic stress disorder—from things he saw and did in Iraq—then he might really do it. He could really shoot us." Her eyes shine with tears and she turns her head away.

I reach over and turn her chin to me.

"Hey—it's gonna be okay," I tell her. Her eyes meet mine, and then she drops her head.

"I actually feel for him," Emery says. "God knows what he's been through over there."

"Listen to you, it's like you're on his side."

"Why does there have to be a side, Jake? He's on our side, remember? He went over there and fought for us so we didn't have to."

"And then he flipped out. Are you saying he should get to keep Patrick?"

"Not now. But would it have come to this if she hadn't tried to take him away?"

"She was afraid of him. Aren't you?"

"Yes, but maybe it didn't have to be this way if he'd gotten the support he needed. You know, Jake, we all have problems. His is called a disorder, mine is called a syndrome, but both of us are dealing with the way emotional stress causes a physical illness. If I hadn't found the right kind of help, I might be just as dysfunctional as he is."

"Don't compare yourself to him," I snap at her. "Those two things are nothing alike."

"It's an extreme viewpoint, I know, but think about it, Jake. There are some parallels, and maybe that makes me more sympathetic to him. I know he's become a monster—I'm terrified of what he might do. But he's also a wounded soldier, and I can't forget that."

Kenji sits up and looks around, rubbing his eyes.

"So what do we do now?" she asks me.

"We wait. Together. We just wait."

My stomach growls and I grab my belly and frown. Kenji grins.

"No, you know what? I'm tired of waiting," I say in a

normal voice. "I'm gonna drive down to Burger King and pick us up some hamburgers." I stand up and reach in my pocket for my keys.

Emery gets this horrified look on her face; it's like she thinks I'm serious. Kenji's eyes open wide, clearly freaked out. Then Emery starts laughing.

"You do that, Biscuit," she says. "Mustard, ketchup, and a pickle for me. Hold the onions."

"Would you like fries with that?" I ask.

Before she can answer, there's noise from the street. It sounds like someone talking on a bullhorn, but it's so muffled, I can't make it out. Stutts stands up and yells at me. "You—turn on the TV. I wanna see what they're saying."

Shit, this sounds like a really bad idea, but I roll the TV on its cart from its spot in the corner and plug it in. I hit the power button and quickly turn down the volume so it won't wake up the kids who are still managing somehow to sleep.

Immediately we're looking at the front of the school. Great. Adrienne Alford, a local reporter, is talking straight into the camera in an end-of-the-world voice that creeps me out.

"What we have here is an active shooter," she says. "A first grade classroom at Lincoln Elementary has been taken over by a gunman who is considered armed and dangerous. As you can see, the area is roped off, and police are on the scene."

It's pretty weird hearing someone say it on TV. I glance at Stutts, but he doesn't react.

"Officials tell us the building has been evacuated—with the exception of four classrooms in the hall where the incident is taking place. That section of the building is on lockdown. We're told the children are locked in their classrooms with their teachers, and they are reported to be safe at this point.

"If you are a parent of a child in the school, you are asked to stay out of the area. Police need your cooperation to ensure the safety of the children. Parents should report to the back parking lot of Mountain Creek Baptist Church near the school for information and instructions. I believe that's on Dogwood Drive."

Stutts watches the screen, and I wonder what's going on in his head.

"The gunman has been identified as Brian Stutts."

Stutts's picture suddenly appears on the screen with his name below. Stutts grunts disapprovingly.

"Police are questioning the gunman's wife, Silda Stutts, and also a man named Tucker Braden, who has contacted the police after seeing the incident on the news. We are told that Braden served with Stutts in Iraq."

"Aw, Tucker," Stutts moans. "What are you doing? Stay out of this."

"And if you're just tuning in, I'll repeat, one man is dead—a security guard named Michael Higgins, and a teacher has been injured."

The security guard, Michael Higgins, is dead!

I knew it on some level, but it slams into me like a Mack truck. I see his face—how it went blank as he gripped his chest and stumbled backward. He looked surprised, and hurt, and confused—all at once.

Stutts goes crazy. "I didn't touch that teacher! You tell them. I didn't lay a hand on her!"

Damn, it's like he didn't even hear that the security guard is dead.

Stutts's loud voice wakes Patrick up. The poor kid grips his pillow and starts rocking.

"Willa Campbell, a first grade teacher at Lincoln Elementary," the reporter continues, "has been taken to Hensonville Hospital. We do not currently have information regarding the extent of her injuries."

"Did Mrs. Campbell get shot?" Rose asks. She's slipped from the back of the room and is standing behind us, listening.

"No, sweetie, that's a mistake," Emery tells her. "You saw Mrs. Campbell when Jake carried her out. She's fine. She's not injured."

"Damn right, she's not injured," Stutts rages. "Those people always get it wrong. You tell 'em—" He breaks off and goes to the door. "You tell them I didn't hurt that teacher," he yells out into the hall. "Make them stop saying that."

He paces back and forth in the middle of the room—the perfect target if sharpshooters have the right angle from the doorway. A part of me wishes they'd take him out now—

stop this bastard from hurting anybody else. But I look at the face of his kid and I know I don't want Patrick to see that.

They wouldn't try it with all these kids in the room, would they? Anything seems possible when *you're* the breaking news.

Emery moves to stand close to me, her face pale. I put my arm around her waist and she lets me.

CHAPTER 21
Emery

Michael Higgins. He had a name, and maybe a girlfriend, or a wife and a kid, a family who will never see him again because he came to help us and Stutts killed him.

He was probably some guy who thought he'd work a cushy job as a security guard at a little elementary school where nothing ever happens. And now he's dead.

Brian Stutts is a murderer—not just someone who's killed in the heat of battle in Iraq, but a murderer who shot a man in cold blood in front of a room full of first graders. He killed a man who was just doing his job—trying to protect little kids from danger.

Jake pulls me to him and I lean into his side. Then he turns the sound off on the TV, which has returned, unbelievably, to regular programming. He rubs his hand lightly across my lower back and my whole body responds to the familiarity of this slight touch.

Poor Simon's actually asleep again. Rose reaches up and hands Lamby off to Jake. She motions for him to come closer and whispers something to him, and he walks back to the front and passes the stuffed animal to Patrick. Patrick grabs it eagerly and hugs it. Jake gives Patrick's head a playful tousle and goes back to sit with the kids.

There's a low buzzing noise, and Stutts reaches into his pocket. He looks at the phone, swears, and throws it across the room. It hits the wall with a bang that makes everyone jump, except Simon, who sleeps on. Jake frowns and opens his mouth to say something, but thinks better of it.

I walk over and pick up the phone. It's remarkably undamaged. I walk back to Stutts and hand it to him. He puts it back in his pocket without looking at it.

"Your wife?" I ask.

"No."

"Tucker?"

He ignores me, still watching the door.

After a long pause, he says, "Tucker needs help. I got nothing to give him."

He looks up at the clock. 12:26.

"I'm tired of being Tucker's mama. He's got problems." At first he doesn't seem to see the irony in this comment. Then: "Yeah, we all got problems."

"What happened to him—over there?"

He reaches up to wipe sweat from his forehead. "You wouldn't understand," he says.

"I want to. To understand."

I glance at Jake. He's sitting on the floor against the back wall near the kids, pretending to doze, but I know he's watching us. The girls whisper to each other.

"People want you to tell it straight, but it doesn't happen straight. It comes at you from all sides, like a tornado. There's no way you can describe it. It's like a bad dream."

I listen without speaking.

"Tucker's not right. Not since that night it happened. It was Tucker. Tucker was the one . . ." He says something I can't hear.

"Tucker was the one who what?"

"Tucker was the one who shot her."

"Who did he shoot?"

"He didn't mean to. It was a mistake. We all make mistakes."

I wait for him to continue. The sun goes behind a cloud and the room turns chilly. And then he begins in a low, urgent voice.

"We were on a cordon and search mission to find the insurgents who attacked our forward operating base the night before. A group of 'em hit our FOB with rockets and mortars, and one of our guys was killed. Gates—he was eighteen. Nice kid, but clueless. Only been in Iraq a few weeks; about as useful as a screen door in a submarine." He shakes his head. "The newbies—they show up in full battle rattle thinkin' they're ready to fight. They're babies."

Stutts glances at the babies in the room like he'd forgotten about them until he said the word.

"That night Gates was killed, he'd left his cell phone in the tent where we bunked, and it rang all night long. Caller ID said *Home*. We knew we couldn't answer. His family had to be notified officially through channels—and if we turned it off, it'd be like telling them. None of us slept at all, listening to that damn phone just ringing and ringing.

"So we were already tired when we headed out. Our platoon leader said we had a pretty good idea of where the attack came from, so about thirty of us rolled out just after midnight. The late night surprise factor gives us the advantage—plus, when it's 110 during the day, you work at night. In our vehicle, it was me and Tucker, a guy named Pitts, and a guy named William P. Jones we called Wimpy."

Stutts is speaking almost normally. It's like he's traveled backward in time to a saner version of himself.

"What makes the heat so bad is you're wearing seventy pounds of gear—body armor with front and rear ceramic plates, 210 rounds of ammo, first aid kit, strap cutter, radio, a seventy-ounce camel pack of water, food, spare batteries, you name it. It's like wearin' a goddamn minivan. Add knee pads and boots, and you don't go anywhere without your weapon; it becomes another appendage. And believe me, once you see a guy lose a chunk of his skull, you're gonna wear that ACH—advanced combat helmet—which is also hot as hell. Tucker used to get his wife to send those girlie minipads to stick inside his helmet for sweat guards."

He smiles at the image, and I smile, too.

"We secured the area that night—about a half a city block—and moved in. Our search of the first two houses turned up nothing but a bunch of scared, angry Iraqis in their pj's." His tone becomes defensive. "Don't look at me like that. I don't like bustin' in people's homes in the middle of the night, but it's the price they pay for freedom. If we want to flush out insurgents, we have to go in where they're hiding, and sometimes that means people gotta lose a little sleep. People besides me."

I wait for him to continue.

"You learn pretty quick not to trust anybody. Old man in the market, kid with a soccer ball—anybody can be hiding a weapon. They'll smile in your face one minute and fire on you the next. I tried to tell Tucker that. He was buddies with all the kids—they came around all the time to see him. I kept tellin' him one of them was going to lob a grenade in the mess hall one day while they were shootin' baskets in that ghetto goal he rigged up."

He runs his hand across his short hair.

"Third house we got to was dark and shadowy, with a small courtyard in front of it. Wimpy said he didn't like the look of it.

" 'C'mon, boys, gotta go out on a limb,' Tucker told us, ''cause that's where the fruit is.' Tucker's always saying crazy stuff, like if a bug hit the windshield of the jeep, he'd say,

'Bet he doesn't have the guts to do that again.' If he caught some guy picking his nose, that was 'digging for gold.' He loved the dumb joke about being stuck between Iraq and a hard place."

Stutts leans forward, focused on his story.

"There were eight in our squad; the other four were in the vehicle ahead of us. Two guys headed around the house to check out the perimeter, and Wimpy, Tucker, Pitts, and I waited for the other two to create the opening. There were some pop shots nearby, so we were jittery—that and no sleep. When they busted down the door, we entered the house.

"Tucker and Pitts took the kitchen, and Wimpy and I moved in fast to the other rooms and rounded up five people—an old man, a teenage boy, a woman, a little kid, and a baby.

"We brought the family in the living room with their hands on their heads. The old man and boy didn't make a sound, but the woman was crying and jabbering at us, and the baby she was holding was screaming. I asked them if they spoke English but got no response.

"Most Iraqis in the villages *don't* speak it, but even if they do, it's almost impossible to get information, because they know what'll happen if they talk. The insurgents need to hide in the villages, so they run their own night raids. They'll go in and kill a family member—sometimes even a child or grandmother—to show their brutality and insure cooperation.

"We shoved them all in the bathroom so we could search the house for weapons. We've done so many of these raids, we can wrap them up pretty quick. You move fast, but the whole time you're ransacking the house, you know that any place you search could be booby-trapped.

"Tucker yelled for me to come in the kitchen. Pitts was holding a plastic food container he'd pulled out of the refrigerator full of wires and plastic pieces. I took the container over to the bathroom, where Wimpy was watching the family from the doorway. 'Who does this belong to?' I yelled at them.

"The teenage boy looked away, and the mother started crying hysterically, dropping to her knees and hanging on Wimpy's pants leg. 'Tie the kid up,' I said. 'We're taking him in.'

"When I got back to the kitchen, Tucker was digging through the trash. He looked up at me to say something, and all of a sudden he wheeled around and aimed his weapon at the open door.

"'Shit!' he yelled, lowering his gun when the red dot of his sight landed on the forehead of a young girl in the doorway. She smiled this big toothy grin and said, 'Hello . . . Tucka . . . USA.'

"'Nahlah, what the hell? You can't just show up like that. You're gonna get killed.'

"'Put your hands on your head,' I yelled at her.

"'It's okay,' Tucker said. 'I know her.'

"'You know all of 'em,' I said. 'Doesn't mean shit.'

"Tucker ignored me and said to the girl, 'Do you live here?'

"'I am living this house,' she said, pointing next door. 'I hear sound while I am sleeping.'

"'Well, go back home,' Tucker told her. 'You don't need to be in the middle of this.'

"'You know the boy who lives here?' I asked. 'About fifteen. Little guy.'

"'Farid, he is my cousin. Farid is good boy,' Nahlah said. 'We are peaceful family. Go USA.'

"'Yeah, well, your peaceful cousin's been building some bad stuff.' Tucker held out the wires.

"'No. These are good people,' she insisted. 'We are peaceful family.'

"Then suddenly the living room erupted in gunfire. And then we were under fire from outside the house. Tucker threw himself on the girl and I hit the floor. He pulled her out of the doorway as I crawled toward it, aiming my rifle around the corner of the frame.

"'Aw, Jesus, she's hit,' I heard Tucker say. I could see people running outside, and there was shouting.

"We heard Pitts yell 'Fuck' from the other room, and Tucker left the girl to crawl toward them. I fired on an attacker fleeing the scene, but he got away. I looked over at the girl. Her eyes were closed, and a dark stain was spreading across her shirt. I thought that she was gone, but then I heard her groan.

"When I got to the main room, Pitts was standing beside

Tucker, who was crouched over Wimpy, lifting the upper half of his body and saying, 'Aw man, aw man, no,' over and over again. A dead Iraqi man was lying near the door.

"The bathroom door was open. All of them were dead—most of them shot in the head, execution style. I turned away from the baby, and I felt the vomit rise in my throat. I moved to Tucker's side. He was talking to Wimpy nonstop. 'Come on, buddy, stay with us. You can do it. Hang in there, Wimpy. I got you, man. You're gonna be okay.'

"'Tucker.' I tried to make him hear me. 'Tucker!' He kept on. 'Tucker, he's gone!' Tucker finally looked up at me, then back at the piece of Wimpy's head that was missing.

"'Come on, Tuck. Pitts, help me carry him out,' I said.

"I could hear gunfire farther down the street where the rest of our platoon had gone, but things had gone quiet on our end, which could be a good sign or a bad one. They carried Wimpy while I covered them. The rest of our squad appeared, and I motioned for them to load Wimpy in their vehicle. I told them I was going back in for the girl and sent Pitts to go find our platoon leader to request permission to take her to a hospital.

"'Nahlah,' Tucker said and turned to go with me.

"'No, man, you stay here. I need you guys to cover me while I bring her out.'

"I crouched low and reentered the house. The girl opened her eyes and looked up at me as I lifted her. She weighed almost nothing, even though she was probably nine or ten years old.

"'It's okay, we're gonna get you some help,' I told her. I'd made it out the front door and was halfway to the vehicle when Tucker opened fire, aiming at something behind me. I wheeled around just in time to see a woman crumple to the ground. Nahlah saw her, too.

"For the rest of my life, I'll hear that scream: 'Ma-maaaa!'

"And then she went limp in my arms.

"I laid the girl on the backseat and ran over to the woman on the ground. I rolled her over and slipped off her head scarf. Sightless eyes stared straight ahead—a beautiful young Iraqi woman. Tucker'd shot her through the neck. I reached for her hand under her skirt to check her pulse and something fell out—a candlestick.

"She was holding a goddamn candlestick. The flame had gone out. All Tucker saw was the glint of moonlight on metal.

"And then Tucker was there beside me, staring at the candlestick. 'She had a gun! She woulda killed you! I saw it! I swear to God, it was a gun . . .'

"I just looked at him. There was nothing I could say. I reached down and closed the dead woman's eyes. Tucker dropped to the ground beside her, with his hands over his head, rocking back and forth and crying, 'Oh God, I killed her. I killed Nahlah's mother.'

"'Tucker, we have to go,' I said, putting a hand on his shoulder. 'You didn't know, man. I would have done the same thing. You couldn't take a chance. You were covering me just like I woulda covered you.'

"It was like he didn't hear me at all.

"'Come on, man,' I said. 'We've got to get the kid to a medic.' There was a US hospital not far away.

"Pitts came around the corner just then with our platoon leader and about a dozen others. 'Nahlah,' I said, trying to get Tucker's attention. 'We've got to help Nahlah.'

"Tucker got up and stumbled, glassy-eyed, to the Humvee and climbed in beside the girl. When he moved next to her, she opened her eyes and started screaming hysterically. As our four vehicle convoy moved out, the yelling turned to whimpering, and at some point she lost consciousness.

"When we got to the hospital, the others carried Wimpy to the morgue and Tucker carried Nahlah's limp body in. The blood had seeped through, covering most of her shirt. Her face was grayish. The doctor took her back. Tucker was a wreck. The doc came out after just a few minutes, shaking his head, to tell us she was gone."

Stutts looks back at the windows, but I know he's seeing Wimpy and Nahlah and Nahlah's mom.

"The hell of it is, I still see that scene every time I lie down to sleep—that little girl in her bloody shirt screaming for her mother, dead because she lit a candle in the dark.

"Tucker never got over it. He felt like he'd killed Nahlah, too."

Stutts turns to me suddenly with an abrupt change of tone.

"Yeah, they train us on our weapons, but there's no training for killing a human being. And when you've taken away the life of a peaceful civilian who turns out to be unarmed, how do you get over that?"

Stutts's voice drops so that I have to lean forward to hear.

"Soldiers make mistakes. Bad shit happens when you put high-powered weapons in the hands of eighteen-year-olds. Killing civilians is part of war. But how do you stop feeling like a murderer?

"Tucker turned to me one night when we were out on patrol, and he asked me what we were doing there—in Iraq.

"I said we came to protect the people from tyranny— and he said no.

"I said we came to honor our beliefs and protect our country—and he said no.

"I said we came to help some rich people get richer, 'cause Tucker was always sayin' it was a rich man's battle but a poor man's fight.

"He said no.

"'What we're doing here,' he said, 'is just trying to stay alive. Our only goal is to make it home.'"

CHAPTER 22

JAKE

I CAN'T HEAR MOST OF THE STORY Stutts is telling Emery, but it seems like he really needs to talk it out, so I try to stay out of it. If anybody can get him to open up, it's Emery. Whether it will help us or not, I just don't know.

I definitely don't like the way he gets so serious, and the way Emery is so caught up in what he's saying. Just when I've had enough of it and I'm about ready to go up there to rescue Emery, Stutts stops talking and drops his head. He wipes his face with the sleeve of his shirt—like the kids do.

And then Emery reaches over and puts a hand on his shoulder. What is she thinking? I stand up and cross the room in three seconds flat.

Stutts looks up at me and says in a low voice,

"I've seen the way you look at me, the two of you. You want to know if I'd hurt kids? There's your answer. We've killed children. Both sides have killed children. I'm a baby killer.

"You know what?" He jabs his finger at Emery and I reach out to pull her away from him. "You just gotta learn to deal with it, when your ideals and principles get in the way of some little kid's right to live. Grenades can't always be aimed. Rockets miss their mark sometimes."

He looks over at Patrick, then at the kids on the carpet. "That's why they can't trust you with your own kids any- more. That's why Tucker's only allowed to visit his kid with a social worker in the room. You believe that shit? A god- damn stranger has to watch him with his own kid. That's what happens when you ask for help. A few weeks in the psych ward, and you're an unfit parent for life. You tell 'em what you're *really* thinking and they'll take your whole family away from you. Forget trying to get help. You'll wind up with nothing!"

He pauses, chest heaving, then looks over at the televi- sion. Suddenly, he's yelling, "Turn it up, turn it up!" He jumps up and runs toward the TV, punching buttons in a panic. "How do you turn this thing up?"

I follow him across the room. On the screen there's a man's face I've never seen.

"Who is it?" I ask.

"I *said* turn it up!" Stutts yells.

A caption appears below the photo. It says TUCKER BRADEN.

"His friend," Emery says to me.

". . . and we're told that Braden was a friend of Brian Stutts, the gunman who is holding first grade students hostage at Lincoln Elementary. The two of them apparently served together in Iraq."

Stutts's face goes still. None of us missed the reporter's use of past tense.

"Again, we've just received word that Tucker Braden was found dead minutes ago by his ex-wife, Julia Braden, in his car in front of her house, shortly after being questioned by police in conjunction with the taking of hostages at Lincoln Elementary by Brian Stutts, who served with Braden in Iraq. Braden, who was under psychiatric care since returning from Iraq, was apparently a victim of a self-inflicted gunshot wound to the head. Police are investigating his suicide and looking for any possible connection with events unfolding at . . ."

The rest is drowned out by the awful sound that Stutts makes. It's like the howl of a wounded animal, terrible to hear. "No, no, noooo," he says, both hands covering his head like he's fending off a blow. "Tucker, noooooo!"

The shit has hit the fan now.

"Tucker! Oh God, no!" he yells, bending over and gripping his gut like he's been punched.

For the first time, his grip on the gun is loosened. I step toward it, but Emery reaches out to stop me and I realize it's too dangerous with him in this state.

"I didn't answer," Stutts moans, sinking into a chair, his face all twisted. "I didn't answer the phone."

"You can't blame yourself," Emery says. "I'm sure—"

"Then who should I blame?" he screams at her in a rage. "Whose fault is it if it's not mine? That's what's wrong with this country. Everybody always blames somebody else!"

Emery moves toward Patrick, who's awake and crying, terrified.

"I didn't do shit for him! No! By God, I'm owning this! *I'm* the one who turned my back on him. Tucker was my friend and I walked away."

And before anyone can move to stop him, he lifts his arm in one swift motion—and points the gun at his own head.

With every ounce of power I can muster, I dive for Stutts and the gun, my head filled with the picture of Patrick watching his dad blow his brains out in front of his eyes. I can't let that happen.

I charge into Stutts full bore, using all my weight to tackle him, my arm reaching up to try to knock his hand away. His chair flies backward with the force of my attack, and I land on top of him. Both of us are rolling on the floor.

I've got to get to the gun. Keep it pointed away from Emery. From the kids. Stop him from pulling the trigger.

He tries to push me off with his left arm, but I cling to his right biceps, pulling myself upward, fighting to grab the gun as he holds it out of my reach. He locks his arm around my neck, but I hang on with everything I've got.

I'm vaguely conscious of Emery moving closer to us, reaching toward Stutts, and I shout at her to get back.

I fight to stay attached, stretching my arms toward Stutts's hand. I get both hands around his wrist and hang on. I twist it so that the nose of the pistol points at the ceiling.

And then, miraculously, I feel my fingertips touch it. Both of us grapple for the weapon. My hand closes around his fist, and I can feel him losing ground as I pull it toward me.

And then he elbows me in the chest, hard, with his free arm, and I feel the air leave my lungs. I make one last lunge for the gun and pull his hand down hard toward me. The last thing I see is the nose pointed downward. I'm looking down the barrel of Stutts's gun. Then the world explodes, and a white-hot pain sears my chest.

CHAPTER 23
Emery

It all happens so fast.

Stutts's howling wakes up Patrick and I go to comfort him. Before I can reach him, I watch in terror as Stutts points the gun at his own head.

Then Jake lunges at Stutts, knocking his chair to the ground. Jake rolls on the floor with Stutts, reaching for the gun. In slow motion I watch, helpless, as the gun turns toward Jake. Time stops, and then . . . and then I feel the blast with my whole being as Jake is knocked backward and falls limp to the floor. I scream, unable to move. *No, oh Jake, no! Please, God, no, not Jake!*

What happens in the next second is a blur.

There is a sudden flash of movement below me.

Something streaks past me on the floor.

Mr. Worley.

The tiny animal darts out into the hall, and before I can stop him, Patrick jumps up from his seat and dives into the hallway after the hamster.

A shot rings out, and I watch in horror as Patrick, little Patrick, collapses in a small heap on the hallway floor, motionless.

"Paaatriiick!" Stutts screams. He lunges into the hall, propelled through the air by terror and grief, gun still in hand. Another shot echoes through the stunned silence, reverberating through the building. I watch as Stutts's body twists sideways, suspended in the air. Then he falls beside his son.

CHAPTER 24
JAKE

I FLOAT THROUGH THE VELVET DARK-
ness, peaceful and warm. I hear distant voices, but I
can't make out their words; I don't feel connected to
them.

And then the lightness of being is gone and my
body feels massive. I'm tired. So very tired . . .

I feel someone rocking me and at first I think it's
my mother.

And then I think it's Emery.

And then both of them are holding me and their
tears wet my face.

CHAPTER 25
Emery

Patrick is down and Stutts is down and Jake is bleeding in my arms. Then the police and paramedics rush in and strap Jake to a stretcher and I can't see him. I can't see if he's okay. I sit crumpled on the floor until they lift me up and walk me out to an ambulance. They drive through the crowds of parents and reporters and policemen to the hospital, and I want to see Jake, but they tell me they have to check me out. And then my mom is there, and she tells me Patrick is okay and Jake is in surgery.

There's so much I want to say to him. And I don't know if I'll ever see him alive again.

I feel like I'm suffocating. There's a hole in my chest, too. I can't lose Jake. Not now.

Finally they come and they tell me Jake is all right, and I start crying and I can't stop.

After what seems like hours, the doctor releases me and they let me go to Intensive Care to be with him. He's pale and he's unconscious, but he's stable, they tell me.

I pull a chair close to his bed so that I can see the rise and fall of Jake's chest. I feel my breathing fall into the same pattern, as if I'm breathing for him. It's dark when he finally wakes up and sees me there beside him and squeezes my fingers.

Maybe Stutts was right. You can't truly see what's good in your life without a reminder of how easily you could lose it. And I'm not going to spend one more minute letting yesterday's anger rob me of today's happiness.

CHAPTER 26

JAKE

I OPEN MY EYES AND EMERY IS THERE.
She's wrapped in a blanket in a chair beside me—
leaning on my bed, holding my hand.

There's a tube running out of my side. A shaft
of fire shoots through my shoulder when I reach
for it.

"That's a chest tube," she says. "They'll take it
out after a few days."

Chest tube? What the hell?

"I know it's uncomfortable, but try not to mess
with it. They had to reinflate your lung."

My lung? Emery's image blurs and I blink to clear
the fog in my head.

"Are you hurting?" she asks. "How bad is it?"

Bad. Real bad. No one's ever set me on fire
before, but I'm pretty sure this is what they call a
ten out of ten.

"Do you want me to get your dad?" she asks.
"He just stepped out in the hall."

I try to speak but all that comes out is a hoarse croak. I look over at the window; it's dark outside.

"You're at Hensonville Hospital. The doctors say you're gonna be fine, Jake."

Fine. I'm gonna be fine. There are tubes and wires and bags and machines. And I definitely don't feel fine.

"Do you remember what happened today?" Emery asks.

I try to focus. And then it starts to come back. There was a gun. I was rolling on the floor with . . .

Stutts. Stutts! I remember.

"You were shot in the chest. The bullet just nicked a lung, and you're in ICU." Emery's voice catches. I squeeze her hand. "You were in surgery for over an hour. But the doctors say you'll make a full recovery. Oh, Jake, we were so lucky it missed your heart. And that it didn't hit any of the kids."

The kids! I reach for the bed rail. Pain shoots through my body, and Emery grabs my arm.

"The kids are fine, Jake. All of them. They're all with their parents. Mrs. Campbell's good, too; she called earlier to check on you—and to say how proud she is of us. And Patrick's gonna be okay. He's here. His mom's with him."

"Patrick?" I whisper.

"Oh God, I'm sorry," she says. "I forgot you didn't know about Patrick."

She brings her face close to mine and speaks slowly. "After you were shot, Mr. Worley ran out into the hall."

Mr. Worley—the hamster.

"Patrick dove after him, and the police—it was a rookie cop, a young guy—fired at him."

The cops shot Patrick?

"What happened was, the cops were moving in because they felt like they were running out of time. They heard the blast when you got shot—"

The gun—it was aimed at me.

"—and this young cop," she says, "the new guy, panicked. When he saw someone streak out into the hall, he just fired."

It's all so fuzzy. Patrick got shot?

"Thank God the guy's not a very good shot. The bullet just grazed Patrick's head. He has a concussion, and they're keeping him here overnight for observation."

I can't follow it all. I lie still for a few minutes, trying not to think about all the places I hurt, and I feel myself drifting off.

Then my dad is standing over me.

"Jake, thank God you're okay!"

He lays his hand on my arm and touches my shoulder like he's trying to make sure all the pieces of me are there. His eyes are red and his clothes are wrinkled and stained. Is that blood on his shirt?

"I don't know what I'd do if I lost you, too," he says in a strangled voice.

Emery's smiling at me. She hasn't looked at me that way in a long time.

"Emery told us what happened," he says. "You were so brave, Jake—too brave."

Did my dad just call me brave?

"You should never have—" He stops and looks away. "He could have killed you. He almost did. But I know you did what you had to do, for the kids. I'm proud of you, son." He pauses. "Your mother would be proud of you, too."

My eyes are stinging and there's a lump in my throat.

Dad pulls himself together. He's back in mayor mode. "I'm sad for his family, of course, and for the family of the security guard. Their deaths are a great tragedy, but it could have been so much worse."

I frown at Emery. Did he say Stutts is dead?

"Stutts didn't make it," she says.

"Did I . . . ?" I whisper.

"No, you didn't shoot him, Jake. After the gun went off and you were shot, then Patrick was shot," Emery says, spelling it out like she's talking to a first grader, which I appreciate in my drug haze. "And when Stutts saw Patrick down, he ran out into the hall. He still had the gun in his hand, and they shot him. They felt like they had to take him down after—after they heard the shot he fired when you went down. They weren't sure what he might do.

"The kids—they didn't see what I saw, thank God," she says, tears starting up again. "I don't think he meant to shoot you. I'm not sure. I think the gun went off accidentally, but I just don't know. It all—it all happened so fast," she says. "It's kind of a blur to me, too. We can talk about it later, when you're not on pain meds."

Pain meds. So foggy.

"You just have to take it slow for a while. No more heroics for a while, Biscuit."

Heroics? Me? My dad's phone buzzes and he steps out of the room.

"Jake?" Emery reaches over and turns my face toward her.

She's looking at me with those green eyes shining, like she can see way past this bed and this room.

"Thank you," she whispers.

I'm confused, but it's a good confusion.

"For what you did. For Patrick. For the kids. For me."

I try to shrug and the pain is blinding. Must remember not to move.

"And for this," she tells me.

I look at the paper she's holding. It looks like my writing.

"It's the letter you wrote me."

Oh—that letter.

"I never got it, Jake. Until today."

I frown, confused.

"I remembered you said something while we were there in the classroom about a letter, so when Tab called to check on me, I told her," Emery says. "She admitted she had it. She took it off the windshield of my car the night you left it."

What? Tab? I don't get it.

"She says she knew how much you hurt me. And she

knew I really liked you." Her face turns pink—God, she's so beautiful—and she drops her eyes. "She figured you were trying to make things right. She was afraid I'd go back to you, and she didn't think I should."

Tab! I hurt too much to be mad right now . . . but I've got a few choice words for that girl.

"I know. I'm really mad at her. I honestly don't know if we can still be friends after this. But she thought she was doing the right thing. Tab's like that. She thinks she knows what's best for everybody." She shrugs. "At least she didn't open it."

She smiles. Aw, man, that smile is killer.

"I found the pieces of the picture inside the envelope— the one you took of us in art class that day, the one I tore up at my locker. I can't believe you picked them up and saved them."

She looks happy—a good sign. I open my hand and close it again over hers.

"I've missed you," she whispers. "A lot."

The curtain opens and my dad comes in. He sees me holding Emery's hand and clears his throat. "I, ah, just wanted to see if you need anything," he says.

"We're good." Emery smiles at him. She doesn't pull her hand away.

Suddenly, there's a commotion to my left as the curtain is yanked aside and The Christine comes barreling into my little cubicle.

"They told me only two visitors, and I told that nurse I

am his stepmother and I have a right to be here. She does not know who she's dealing with."

"Ma'am." A young nurse is right behind her. "I'm sorry, but you'll have to . . ."

Emery's fighting to keep a straight face.

"She can take my place," Dad says. "Come on in, honey; I'll wait in the hall for a bit."

"No, no, I'm just leaving," Emery says, standing up. "She can have my spot."

"Don't," I whisper, reaching out to hold on to her.

She leans down to put a hand on my shoulder.

"I promised Mom I wouldn't stay too long. She's in a panic, as you might imagine. Doesn't want to let me out of her sight. I'm supposed to call her to come pick me up, but I'll be back tomorrow. You get some rest. After you visit with Th—Christine."

She gives me an *oops* look after she almost says *The*. I wink at her, and she blows me a kiss and pulls aside the curtain to leave.

CHAPTER 27

Emery

I push the lobby button in the elevator and lean against the wall. My legs wobble a little as I walk across the lobby; I hadn't realized how tired I am.

A sign above an archway says CHAPEL. In the dimly lit room beyond it, a dark-haired woman kneels alone near the front, her head bowed.

I know instinctively who she is.

I step into the room, move quietly past the three rows of church pews, and kneel beside her.

She looks up at me. Her face is streaked with tears. A rosary is threaded through her long graceful fingers.

"Are you Silda?" I ask.

"Yes?" she whispers.

"I'm Emery Austin," I tell her, not sure if my name will mean anything to her.

Before I can say more, she reaches out and

takes my hand in both of hers. Her hands are cold, but her grip is strong.

"Thank you," she says with a slight accent; she's pretty and soft-spoken.

"I didn't want to disturb you—"

"No, I wanted to meet you. My baby—my Patrick tells me you gave him hugs. I'm so, so sorry for what . . ." She begins to cry.

"Is Patrick okay?" I ask.

She nods, and when she can speak again, she asks, "Are you all right?"

"I'm fine."

"And the boy—"

"Jake. Jake's fine, too."

"I'm thanking God for sparing Patrick's life. And I am praying for him to have mercy on my husband's soul."

"I'm so sorry you lost your husband."

"I lost Brian months ago," she says quietly, "in a place far from here. I wish . . . I wish I'd tried harder to help him," she says. "I didn't know . . ."

"No one could have seen what would happen."

"No." She shakes her head.

"It was obvious that he loved you very much," I tell her. I'm not sure how much I should say. "Even the way he said your name . . ."

Her face crumples and she nods. "I wish you could have known Brian—in happier times. He was a good person."

She wipes her face with her hand and says, "I'm afraid Patrick won't remember him. He's so young. I wish he could remember what his father was like—before—"

"He will," I tell her. And I know I'm right. "He'll remember his dad. He'll remember the good days."

I reach out and hug her. There doesn't seem to be anything more to say.

"Oh," she says as I'm standing up to leave, "he gave me something to give to you or Jake—Patrick did."

She reaches in her purse and hands me a small stuffed animal—Lamby. Lamby with a tiny bloodstain right across his heart. He must have made the trip to the hospital in the ambulance with Patrick.

"I don't know how you did it," she says. "Stayed calm for the children."

"They're great kids," I answer, my voice cracking a little. "I couldn't let them down."

I dig in my purse for a Kleenex as I walk back out to the lobby.

Suddenly, my legs nearly give way and I drop into a chair near the front door, clutching the stuffed animal and trying to pull myself together.

It hits me—hard—that I saw two men die today. Witnessing Michael Higgins's death and Brian Stutts's death has changed me in ways I don't even understand yet. And changed their family's lives forever.

A line from a Dylan Thomas poem comes to me: "After the first death, there is no other." Death can never again be an abstract concept to me. It feels like nothing else will ever have the same impact. Like Stutts said—I know things now I didn't know before.

The tears flow and I let them. People walking past try not to look. They're probably used to crying here.

The only thing that's keeping me from coming completely unhinged is knowing I can talk to Jake about it.

My phone dings and I pull it from my purse. *need u* the somewhat blurry text says.

Apparently, Jake got his phone back.

I smile, blow my nose on the wadded-up tissue, and scroll back to an earlier message I've read three times. *Emery, call me. Worried sick. Please let me know you're all right. Dad.* I texted him as soon as I got my phone back and saw his message. It's a number I didn't have, but one I plan to call later, when I have lots of time to talk.

And then there are the texts from Mom—a dozen or so—from panicked pleas for reassurance that I'm okay to more recent orders for me to come home and get some rest.

And then I make a decision, feeling for the first time in a while like the master of my own fate. Mom'll just have to deal with waiting for me a little longer tonight.

I know I need rest. But for the first time in a long while, I'm fine.

Just fine, Valentine.

I tuck my phone back in my purse and my hand brushes the photograph. I take out the picture Jake took on the first day we talked in art class—now made up of a dozen jagged squares held together with Scotch tape. I smile at our unsuspecting faces—all happy and innocent and hopeful.

All the pieces were still there—ready to be put back together in the spaces where they belonged. I turn away from the door and walk to the elevator that will take me back to Jake.

ACKNOWLEDGMENTS

I CAN'T BEGIN TO DESCRIBE HOW LOVELY IT IS to work with my Penguin editor, Nancy Paulsen, who felt like a soul sister from our first conversation. I admire her passion for bringing great books to a diverse population of readers, and I respect her judgment in all things. Her expert guidance benefitted this book enormously; she is a writer's dream editor.

Words are inadequate to convey my gratitude to Jill Corcoran, my wonderful agent at Herman Agency. I will always love her for announcing on Twitter that she'd just found a diamond in the slush pile—at a time when I was starting to feel like a writerly lump of coal. Her enthusiasm and energy inspire me to write more and better. Jill is the perfect blend of wit and wisdom.

My daily life is enriched beyond measure by my inner circle. I am so thankful for my husband, David; my mom, Martha Brigman; and my family, Drew McDowell, Emily McDowell Elam, Cason Elam, and the always entertaining Jack Elam, for their faith, enthusiasm, editorial advice, and technical expertise. They are the heart and soul of everything that's good in my life.

My sister Susan Siniard's delight in the accomplishments of others is generous and genuine; she's an amazing nurturer of family talent—mine included. Her husband, Tommy, is "practically blood kin," as we say in the South, and has done more for our family than I can say. My sister Julie Moreau shares the family writing genes; I'm grateful for her insightful suggestions and NOLA hospitality. My brother, John, knows how to do most anything and helps us keep our lives in order. Close friends Geoff and Emily Evans, Megan Mercier, and Hannah Cail have played key roles in my writing path and are loved and appreciated "family" members, too.

For this work I'm indebted to Christopher George for his generous gift of time and friendship in helping me understand some of the nuances of a soldier's life. Many thanks are due to my cousin Jeanne Wilson, a beloved first grade teacher, for wonderful stories from the trenches. Thanks also to Wendy Stephens, dear friend and talented librarian. I hope I did half the job she does of matching kids to books when I was in the classroom. And Shari George deserves thanks for being such an enthusiastic force on the hometown team from the very beginning. I love her amazing energy.

Many friends have lifted me up when I needed it. Thank you, Jim Sherwood, Jerry Whitworth, Beth and Walter Thames, Lula Mae Martin, Mike Chappell, Mike Patton,

Michael Walker, Nichole Liese, Dena and Barry Schrimsher, Jerry Barclay, Carol Dayton, Turner Moore, Ben Morehead, Shaw Bowman, Alice Evans, Michael Kamback, Andrew Cotten, Russell Goldfinger, and Aaron Byers. And thanks to Raymond Harrell, Zach Hagin, and Jordan Hall for the great work on NotRequiredReading.com.

I doubt I would have ever written a word without the encouragement of wonderful hometown mentors R. A. Nelson (*Teach Me*, *Breathe My Name*, *Days of Little Texas*, and *Throat*) and Hester Bass (*The Secret World of Walter Anderson*). And I owe much to the Southern Breeze chapter of the Society of Children's Book Writers and Illustrators. "Join SCBWI" was some of the best advice I heard as a beginning writer.

AUTHOR'S NOTE

IF YOU SUFFER FROM POST TRAUMATIC STRESS disorder (PTSD)—whether you're a military veteran, victim of a natural disaster, sufferer from domestic abuse, or a survivor of an act of terrorism or other trauma—there are trained counselors in your area who can help you. You can access these professionals online or through your local doctor or mental health center. Please seek treatment; let others help you find the strength to rebuild your life.

Postural orthostatic tachycardia syndrome affects 1 in 100 teens. If you feel you may have POTS symptoms, seek medical help. Insist on a thorough examination for any physical or psychological problem you're experiencing, and see other doctors if you don't get satisfaction from your current ones. Trust your instincts when your body says something's wrong, and be persistent in seeking answers. It's a very manageable condition once you understand the symptoms.